TAMALES WITH FRIENDS

A CHRISTMAS CELEBRATION OF THE LADIES OF SEA FOAM LANE

EVA HERNÁN

THE SEA FOAM LANE SERIES
BOOK ONE

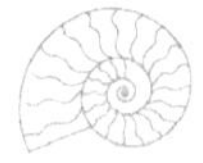

ISBN: 978-1-952004-16-2

Cover design and interior design by Cate Lumière

Cover and author photograph by Cate Lumière

Copyediting and Proof Reading by William Linus

For inquiries about this book, please e-mail:
Inquiries@BlueSandPublications.com

www.BlueSandPublications.com
www.EvaHernan.com

Santa Monica
Long Beach
Palos Verdes
San Pedro
Santa Catalina Island

Bonnie
&
Emma
Miriam
Sea
Foam
Lane
Susy
Lesley
Frances

A Christmas celebration of the ladies of Sea Foam Lane

Eva Hernán

*This book is dedicated to all the grandparents and parents
that have shared their cooking traditions with their children
and grandchildren!*

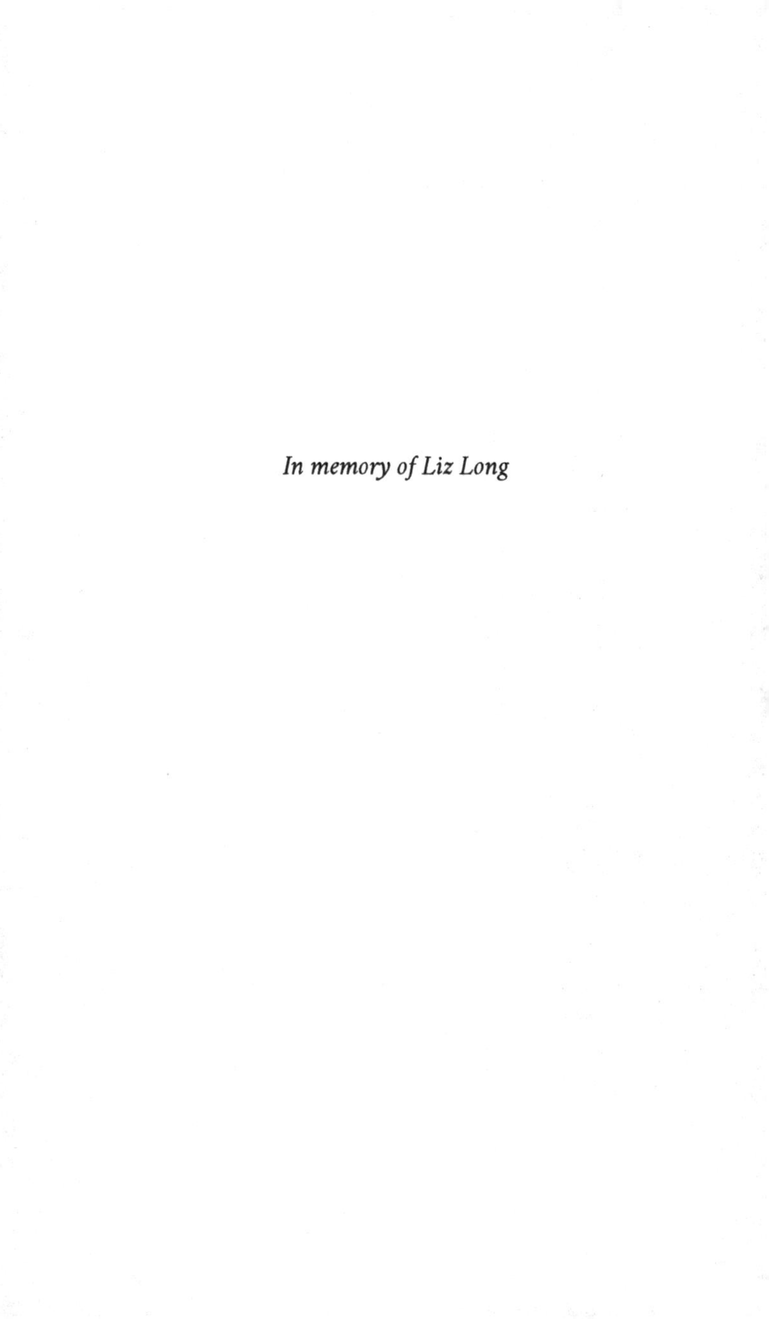

In memory of Liz Long

INTRODUCTION

Nestled in one of the oldest neighborhoods of the eclectic coastal community of San Pedro, there is a picturesque cul-de-sac, Sea Foam Lane. Six lovely ladies live in the five beautiful homes built between the 1930s and 1940s. The houses are representative of the boom times of this enclave of Los Angeles County. Five of the inhabitants of the charming cul-de-sac have seen San Pedro transform from a fishing town to one of the busiest ports in the world without losing its multicultural heritage. They have been calling this peaceful street home for years. Then there is Susy, the sixth lady at Sea Foam Lane, who just moved in over a year ago. For the first time its habitants are getting together to celebrate Christmas.

Each one of the houses on Sea Foam Lane is unique just like their owners.

The first house, at the left of the cul-de-sac, is owned by Lesley and it is a perfect example of ranch architecture, with an L shaped single level floor plan. Fragrant red roses follow the contour of the house, providing a contrast to the impeccably painted cream exterior. Lesley is sixty-five years old and lives alone after having lost her husband in 2015. While she lives by herself, she is not lonely because her family lives in town and during the weekdays she takes care of her six grandchildren. You can see Lesley driving a big SUV around town, taking the grandchildren to schools, events and appointments. She wanted to be a full-time grandmother but somedays she questions what she wished for. There are days when she does not have a minute of respite. During the weekdays Lesley is in charge of her grandchildren from the moment she picks them up to take them to school, until the time their parents show up to take them home. But she will not have it any other way, and being busy keeps away her memories of the bakery she used to own—"The Sweet Breeze." She loved her bakery, but after the death of her husband and the lack of interest in the business from her children, she sold it. She does not miss waking up early in the morning to start baking, but she misses the interaction with loyal customers, preparing cakes for special occasions, and the smell of the French bread coming out of the oven. She still enjoys baking cookies, pastries and cakes to share with the rest of the inhabitants of the cul-de-sac, and baking for different fundraisers. Lesley moved to this house twenty years ago when she and her husband decided to downsize after becoming empty nesters when the last of the kids left to college. While this house is smaller than her prior home, the kitchen is enormous. There are plenty of rooms for when the grandchildren are around, and a dream backyard for the kids to play.

Next to Lesley is Miriam. Never married, she is sixty-three years young, full of energy and drives a flashy red sports car. Miriam's house is a classic Craftsman style structure, with a beautiful front porch framed by thick tapered columns and the low pitched roof. If Miriam is not entertaining friends at home, she is taking dancing classes, playing tennis, cooking, going to golf lessons, or on cruises traveling to different regions of the globe. She worked in investment banking, toiling in mergers and acquisitions and retired when she was fifty-five because she wanted to start living. Infamously, Miriam made history during her farewell dinner for having said "I have been working my derriere off in this industry for thirty years and so far, I have not found a store that sells time. Therefore, ciao, life is too short to be here." Miriam understands that time is limited, every day is precious, and every second is something we cannot get back. She lives each moment to its fullest and her bucket list keeps getting empty, just to be re-filled with more things to do before she departs from this world. She arrived in the neighborhood ten years ago.

After Miriam's house and at the end of the street, the sisters Emma and Bonnie have been sharing a simple two story Colonial style house for the last fifteen years. The house was originally owned by one of the current habitants of Sea Foam Lane. Emma and Bonnie usually introduce themselves as Mrs. Stevens (Emma) and Miss Rogers (Bonnie), a habit from their days as elementary school teachers. Both are in their mid-seventies. Emma has been a widow for seventeen years and shortly after losing her husband, she and Bonnie decided to buy the house with the biggest front and back yards and the greatest square footage on the street. The house was ideal for giving private tutoring lessons when they left the classrooms, but after five years as private tutors they decided it was time to be retired for good and spend their hours on their second passion—gardening. If they are not working in their garden, then they are reading and knitting. They love to read books with stories that have a gardening component; they have devoured the "Wildflower Series" by Elizabeth H. Long. You can find them every morning taking care of the seasonal and perennial plants in their front yard. They used to volunteer in the local botanical garden until a year ago, when driving became one of their least favorite activities. Bonnie lost the love of her life in the Vietnam War, and she never fell in love again.

In the Spanish Colonial Revival home next to Bonnie and Emma lives Susy, the only one of the ladies of Sea Foam Lane that is not even close to forty, and every weekday goes to work. She is as a project director for one of the aerospace companies in the city of El Segundo. She has a cat and a dog, the only pets in the cul-de-sac. Originally from Wisconsin, Susy got an internship in a local company. After graduation she had several offers to work in the area around El Segundo. She relocated to Los Angeles and has not missed the Midwest winters. Susy is the new kid on the block. She arrived in the summer of 2017, when she decided to buy her first house. She fell in love with the area, and the house had everything she was looking for except proximity to work. This could be overlooked since she feels transported to a begone era every time she opens the door, takes off her shoes and walks barefoot over the original hardwood floors. Somehow it washes away whatever happened during the day at work.

Next to Susy is Frances, she is sixty-four years old. Frances is the inhabitant of Sea Foam Lane that has lived the longest on the cul-de-sac. She arrived on the street when she and her husband Mark bought the house that now Bonnie and Emma call home. Frances still remembers with joy when she opened the red door to her first house. She was happily married to Mark for a little over a year and was pregnant with their first child. Mark and Frances raised their family in the two-story house and stayed there until the little cottage on the corner was for sale. That is when they decided to downsize and buy the house. Frances has been a widow for the last five years. Her four children are scattered across the country; and they come to visit once per year when she is lucky. She says her kids think if they video call her often, then there is no need to visit because they get to see her on a screen. She does not care too much for the calls because it is always a three ring circus when they call her—the younger grandchildren running around screaming out of control, the teenagers showing their faces in the screen for a second and walking away, their dogs barking and the phones of her kids ringing nonstop. She spends her days watching old movies and lately decluttering her house. She is not a pack rat, but decided it was time to let go of family memorabilia and the antique furniture after having made multiple attempts to have her kids take what they wanted. Frances holds the record of living on the street: forty years! She can not imagine living somewhere else that is not this street where some of her happiest memories happened.

NEWFOUND JOY FOR THE HOLIDAYS!

Friday, December 21, 2018

FOR SUSY ANDERSON it has been a long time since she has enjoyed the last few days of the year at home, no traveling or having to go to the office to finish a special assignment or trying to get a head start on a new task. She hasn't felt this light and happy when leaving the office in a long time. Maybe knowing that she doesn't need to be back on Monday has put a smile on her face. For the last two years she has been working on special projects nonstop. First she was assigned to a project considered the hot potato of her division; a project that had burned out several experienced senior project managers. For months the monumental assignment deprived her of many hours of sleep, but at the end it got Susy her first promotion, to director. Besides the promotion, she gained the recognition of all her peers in the El Segundo aerospace engineering community. But with success came more challenging tasks. She has only been able to take a few scattered days off for medical appointments and to deal with personal stuff, but never coming close to taking a week off until now, when she decided to be gone from the office until January third. Not quite two weeks off, but Susy thinks it is a great way to end 2018 and start the new year.

For a Friday, traffic is almost non-existent. Usually, the second half of December is a good one for commuters in Southern California. With schools on Christmas vacation, people traveling, or people just taking the last days of the year off to stay at home, it reduces the number of cars on the freeway significantly. Susy is amazed there is hardly anybody on the Santa Diego Freeway or the 405 like most Angelenos refer to it. It seems everybody has already taken the day off in anticipation of the holiday week. She is not surprised if people left the office early to go shopping. This week several of her coworkers have been skipping lunch to leave at two o'clock and get to the shopping centers before the afternoon parking mayhem starts. Susy is staying on the freeway, avoiding being near any shopping center, and she intends to stay away from them the rest of the year. She is going straight home to start enjoying her long overdue time off.

As she takes the 405 exit to merge onto the 110 Harbor Freeway, she realizes that she has not stopped smiling since she closed the door to her office. The other thing she notices is that she has been driving over the speed limit for the first time in months, and while she is tempted to step on the gas pedal, she decides it is not worth the risk to herself and others. The speedometer eases to sixty-five miles per hour. She does not want to be pulled over by the Highway Patrol and start her holiday by getting a ticket. Her face suddenly looks younger, like she has lost a year or two. She looks relaxed. Susy is looking forward to spending the last days of the year at home. It is the first time in a while that she is not traveling for Christmas to Wisconsin. 2018 has been wonderful and it is her first full year in her new home!

Since late September she had been looking forward to celebrating Halloween, Thanksgiving, Christmas and the New Year; by the end of September, she was already planning how to decorate the house for Halloween, and she had bags of candy to give away. As soon as the Halloween decorations came down, she put out the Thanksgiving ones; the carved orange pumpkins were replaced with yellow, green and orange little pumpkins; the ghost and skeletons with a couple of scarecrows. She even got some orange leaves made of a silky material attached to thin orange ribbons and hung them out on the porch next to the living room and dining room windows. They moved so graciously with the afternoon breeze, they looked like they were going to fly away, and gave a little extra fall season touch. In the days before Thanksgiving, she went shopping for Christmas decorations. She wanted to buy a Christmas tree so bad the day after Thanksgiving! But she decided to wait a few days and buy a live Christmas tree. A live Christmas tree that she could see grow through the years.

Last year holiday season had not been easy for Susy. The second half of 2017 was an emotional rollercoaster for her.

The week after the 4th of July she broke up with her boyfriend of four years, it was not easy but necessary. Their relationship had become stagnant. He was perfectly happy with the status quo, but Susy felt she was getting stuck in the role of eternal girlfriend. He couldn't understand why she was buying a house away from where she worked and why she was not considering his idea to move in together. An idea only that was triggered when she told him she had made an offer to buy the house she had liked in San Pedro. He had been hinting about wanting to move in together, but it never sounded serious. Susy felt she was going to become his roommate, and everybody knows roommates can come and go. It was time to spend time apart and maybe say goodbye for good.

While she was emotional for weeks after the breakup, by the end of the summer she almost had forgotten about the ex-boyfriend. But it was around mid-October when she started to feel anxious. All of a sudden the memories of the Halloween costumes worn to the parties that they attended, the Thanksgiving dinners they had shared, the Christmas gifts exchanged, and the kisses during the New Year celebrations came rushing to her like the lights of a train in a dark tunnel. She found herself fighting back tears out of nowhere during the least expected moments. But thanks to her family and friends that did not let her become a couch potato eating pints of ice cream indefinitely, she survived the holidays. Her friends and family listened to her and invited her to different activities during late 2017. Susy was able to see that she could have a wonderful time without needing to bring another to Autumn and Winter events. By the end of December, she was able to attend holiday parties without agonizing if she was going to be able to hold back tears. The flow of memories with the "Ex" had stopped, and she did not feel like she was standing in that cold and dark tunnel seeing the light of the train coming at her. She was outside the tunnel.

By January 2, 2018, Susy had beautiful memories of her first holiday season without "the Ex." She had said goodbye to 2017 and was embracing everything 2018 had in store for her.

Her Friday commute is coming to an end and she

can see in the distance the harbor cranes. While they are always illuminated at night, for some reason during the holidays they looked festive. She can see the blue lights of the Vincent Thomas bridge; those lights are always blue, too bad they are not more festive. She reaches the end of the Harbor freeway and now she is driving down Gaffey street. The street has been decorated since late November with the traditional colors of the season, green and red. There is not too much activity on the street and Susy is excited that soon she will be at home. She is ready to make more happy holiday memories, and she still is driving with a big smile.

MYSTERY CAR

*S*unday, December 23, 2018

ANOTHER CLASSIC WINTER morning in San Pedro is waiting for Susy. Golden sunlight breaking through the trees' canopies, a brisk winter breeze and the birds flying from tree to tree. Sometimes she misses the change in the seasons like the ones she experienced in her childhood in Wisconsin. It doesn't hurt to have a little snow around Christmas, but she never enjoyed having to shovel snow all winter. She likes just getting in her car and going to work without the need of getting a workout in the morning before even leaving the driveway. She discovered the beauty of living without snow when she went to college, to a town where it is spring all year long. It is only during the holidays that she misses the weather, only one week of the year. During the other fifty-one weeks she is happy with the mild weather and the pleasant sea breeze she gets to enjoy living in San Pedro. She is thankful for not needing AC or the heater most of the year. She is glad and relieved not to be traveling and just staying at home to relax. This year she wanted to enjoy every minute after leaving the office, and not have to deal with crowded airports, delayed flights and the occasional ice storm. She wanted it to be like those Christmas weeks as a child when the only worry was to convince her mom to allow her to eat few more gingerbread cookies. Now she only has to convince herself to enjoy all the holiday goodies and worry only about going back to her carbs deprived life after the New Year.

Without a boyfriend, her friends not staying in the city for the holidays and her family not visiting, she decided to invite the rest of the ladies of Sea Foam Lane for Christmas. This will be the first time Susy is entertaining since she moved in. It has been over a year since she arrived. It is time to make her debut as a hostess.

After Halloween, Susy thought of inviting her neighbors for Thanksgiving but that was going to be a monumental endeavor, not because the number of people, but because she considerers herself a rookie at preparing a turkey dinner, and the rest of the ladies of Sea Foam Lane have cooked at least forty turkeys each. She was intimidated by their Thanksgiving cooking skills. Susy has become close to the five lovely ladies; they have become family to her. Each one of them is a character in her own right, but then everybody has eccentricities. She was hesitant to invite them for Christmas, thinking they would have plans with their families and friends, but to her surprise they accepted, except one of them.

What is Susy going to prepare for the occasion? The answer: tamales and green *pozole*, two traditional Mexican dishes. She can prepare tamales and other staples of the Mexican cuisine like a pro. Her mom's mom, *Abuelita* (Grandma) Amelia, taught her. Susy and her sisters spent a few summers and holidays with their grandmother in the old family house located in a small town in central Mexico.

Amelia Guzmán was a strong woman. Amelia was left with three young daughters after having lost her husband in a fatal accident in the fields. At the time Emilia, Lucia (Susy's mom) and Patricia were little girls not even teenagers; Emilia the oldest was just nine years old, Lucia seven and Patricia five. Still grieving from her lost, Amelia took over managing the fields while raising her three daughters. After four years of working in the fields, Amelia had the best harvest, that year the weather was perfect. The bountiful harvest had given Amelia a little extra money. She decided to buy pigs, chickens, and bees. A wise decision that paid off in the following years.

The years went by, and Amelia put her three daughters through college. Each time one graduated from high school she would tell her "Your inheritance is the knowledge you will acquire when going to college. That will last you a lifetime and will provide for you."

What Amelia Guzmán never imagined was that one of her daughters, Lucia, while on an exchange with an American university would meet Susy's father, fall in love and get married after graduation. Amelia was not too happy in the beginning. Her unhappiness was immortalized in the wedding pictures where the matriarch of the Guzmán family had an epic scowl on her face. Once Susy asked her mother while going through the family album, why she had kept those pictures showing her grandma Amelia so unhappy and flat out upset. Her mother replied that she left them in the album as a reminder and lesson that people's actions cannot be erased, that words and actions affect others, but most importantly that people can change. Grandma Amelia was unhappy on one of the most important days of her daughter, her wedding, and it had been immortalized.

The relationship between Lucia and Amelia Guzmán started to change when Susy was going to be born. Lucia asked Amelia to be with her at least a week before the delivery date. Reluctantly Amelia took several flights to get from Mexico to Wisconsin. The days before the birth, Amelia's unhappiness started to melt just like a block of ice left out in a hot summer day. By the time of the first contractions, all the resentment she had been harboring because Lucia had left Mexico and got married just out of college was gone. When Susy cried for the first time it was not just the beginning of her life but the rebirth of her mother's and grandmother's relationship. Amelia also stopped seeing Theodore Anderson as the "Gringo" that had stolen her daughter, but as the son she never had. And it is here where I leave you with Susy, who is ready to get out of the house.....

I AM ready to walk out the door to get the last ingredients for my Christmas dinner extravaganza, but I cannot leave yet because somehow I managed to lose my key once again. Nolan, my cat, is perched on the ottoman in the living room looking at me with those blue piercing eyes as I go in circles around the house trying to find it. I am giving up. I will get the spare key. I do not like to do that because if I cannot find the spare key, then I will be in trouble, but I have been looking for it all over the house. I go to the master bathroom and open the medicine chest and open the old tin bandage box where I keep the spare key. As I put the key in the right pocket of my jeans, I can feel the missing key in there. "Ooops!" It has been there all this time. I put back the spare key in the old tin box. I stop to look at it, the layer of white paint is worn off, the metal is exposed on some of the edges and two of the red words have faded away due to the use through the years. Of all my possessions, this is one of my top five favorites. For me it is a family heirloom, it is part of my earliest memories. I still remember my mother taking a bandage from it when I came back from kindergarten with my knees all scratched after falling in the playground and leaving some of the skin of my knee on the cement. Through the years the only constant in my mother's medicine cabinet was this little tin can. She used to change the bandages from the cardboard boxes to the tin can. When my father asked me to help him clear my mother's items from the house after her passing, I took the tin can. Dad was happy I was going to keep it.

Before I leave for the store, I stop and take some deep breaths before I face the crowds in the local grocery. Nolan comes over to rub against my legs, giving the black jeans the classic look of a cat owner. A long time ago I gave up cleaning the hair from my clothes in the house; I do it in the garage before I get in the car. The white furball goes on his merry way, not showing any additional interest in me. He does not care if I am leaving or not. It is time for one of his multiple naps and he is a stickler for his routine.

As I open the back door, Roland, my black Labrador, greets me as I step out of the house into the crisp air. He has been playing out in the backyard all morning. He likes to look at the birds and growl at the blue jays when they try to come to the planters to hide the peanuts they got from other houses. My neighbors and I have bird feeders, but we do not feed them peanuts. We have a good number of visiting birds, and also squirrels that always find a way to get to the bird food.

"Roland, come on boy, you need to get inside the house. Mom is going to the supermarket." Roland goes inside as soon as I point that he needs to go in. Either he is obedient, or he knows he will get his morning snack.

I close the door behind me. I want to take a look at the plants on the side of the house. As I make my way through the narrow cement pathway, I can see I have several hours of gardening ahead of me, my small plants need some love and care. I do not have a large variety of plants like my neighbors do. In the backyard there are several mature bougainvillea, a Meyer lemon tree and rose bushes, which were here when I bought the property. The side of the house has a strip of dirt next to the wooden fence that separates my house from Bonnie and Emma's. There were a few empty pots scattered over the strip when I moved in, surrounded by mint and ice plant. Per Bonnie and Emma's recommendation, I planted geraniums in the empty pots. I wanted plants that did not require too much care. In the front yard there is a jacaranda tree, two sago palms framing the path from the sidewalk to the front door, and rose bushes providing color. As I made my way along the side of the house, I notice I need to spend some time this holiday break tending the geraniums. There are dry flowers and leaves that need to be removed. I reach the front yard and I see the pain of my gardening existence, there is the bare patch of dirt next to the fence with Bonnie and Emma's house, under the Jacaranda tree where the grass refuses to grow. I was told the prior owners were not successful at growing anything there. Before I return to the office, I am going to put decorative pebbles and pots with flowers there. I tried already long enough to see if I had the magic touch to bring the patch to life and it has been futile. I believe even Emma or Bonnie could not do anything for this bare patch, not even they with the greenest thumbs on the street.

To my surprise I find the rest of the of the inhabitants of Sea Foam Lane congregated around a yellow car with racing stripes parked in front of my house.

"Hello ladies!" I greet my neighbors. They are looking at the car like it is a spaceship that just has dropped from the sky. It is a muscle car with a nice yellow paint job. I do not understand what the big interest is, unless there is a dead body inside. They reply, "Good Morning, Susy", "Hello dear."

"What do we have here?" I inquire, hoping to understand what the big fuss is about.

"It's not yours?" Frances asks me right away.

"No, it is not mine, I am seeing it for the first time, and I do not think Santa brought it to me as a present." If this car were mine, it would not be parked on the street, it would be in the garage away from the sunlight and away from the jacaranda trees to avoid anything landing on top of it. The owner is lucky the jacaranda trees on our block are not in bloom, otherwise his car would be covered with purple flowers in no time.

Bonnie, who is the most serious of all, says in a calm tone but giving her words a little extra emphasis, "This car was left here between 2 a.m. and 6 a.m." Her sister, Emma looks at her, starts shaking her head and replies, "Yes, Bonnie, you know the exact time because you are the owl of the street."

"It is not my fault I cannot sleep." Bonnie replies while giving a harsh look to Emma.

Lesley, who is the calmest of the bunch, says "It looks like the owner is living in the car." To my dismay after a brief silence, she follows the sentence with "Or maybe it is stolen and all the boxes and bags in the back seat are stolen goods."

"Ladies, I do not think it is stolen. I think it belongs to a visitor of one of the houses on the street. Yes, there are a lot of things in the car, but those nicely dry-cleaned shirts lead me to believe the owner of the car has an office job and he maybe is moving to a new place. The car is too clean and new to belong to somebody living in it. And maybe he is a salesman and is always on the run eating in his car, which explains all the fast-food paper bags and the empty water bottles." I tell them after having walked around the car to get a closer look at the exterior and interior. My opinion after my quick inspection does not satisfy my friends. They are looking at me like I said something wrong.

"Well, if the car is not gone by Wednesday, we should call the police and have it towed away. We do not want our street becoming a parking lot." Frances, who has been recuperating from a hip implant replacement, says emphatically.

As everybody shakes their head in agreement, Miriam, who is the more active and energetic one, says that she needs to go to her tennis match. She can't stay longer to make more theories about the mysterious car. She is saying all this as she is walking backwards and all of a sudden gives a little jump and turns around to face her house. I follow suit and inform my inquisitive neighbors that I have to go to the store. I am sure they are going to be there for a while; this is the highlight of their day. I turn around and I open the garage door. As I am getting the car out, to my surprise my friends are going back to their respective houses, they had enough of the mystery car. I exit the cul-de-sac and it seems like yesterday when I arrived in the neighborhood. I remember researching the beach cities close to work. I discovered quickly that my pocket could not afford anything with a decent backyard. I expanded my search parameter few miles and discovered San Pedro. When I saw the posting in one of the real estate websites, I knew it was the right property for me and my furry kids–a backyard, fireplaces, hardwood floors, old charm. I remember driving to see the house and almost when I was getting ready to exit the freeway, I thought the commute was not ideal. I was used to driving a few minutes to work and I could tell it was going to be easy over thirty-five minutes to get to work. That day I arrived to San Pedro few hours before my appointment with the realtor to check the town, and after going through different neighborhoods I knew San Pedro was the place for me. I felt like I had found a gem, the last of the coastal communities with a small-town feel. One of the major selling points of the house was the location. It was on a small cul-de-sac with only five houses on it, and few blocks away from a park. A beautiful park where I could take Roland for a walk or where I could go jogging. It almost reminded me of Central Park, a miniature Central Park. The house did not have an ocean view, but the bluffs where you can see the most wonderful sunsets are just minutes away. In addition, the property was custom built, with details that you do not find in the houses that are built by the hundreds.

When I went to see the house, I fell in love with it. It needed minor repairs, but the hardwood floors were the originals, and lucky for me, the prior owner had covered them with carpet a long time ago. The craftsmanship was amazing; there was wood inlay going around the floor with elaborate designs in the corners. There was a fireplace in the master bedroom and one in the living room. The realtor explained to me that the house was built in the late 1930s. It was custom built, hence the two fireplaces in such a small property. A newlywed couple from the East Coast had it built, and they lived there all their lives. The husband died first, and the wife lived there for another ten years alone. Their nieces and nephews who inherited the property wanted to sell it as soon as possible to divide the proceeds. The realtor commented that I was going to be entertained by my neighbors and that they were a close group. I did not ask him the reason for the comment. I decided to buy the house and meet the neighbors later. The size was right for one person with two pets, and it was a private place. Since the day I arrived in El Segundo for my internship, I fell in love with the Spanish Bungalows that you see in different parts of the city. My dream of owning an old Spanish style house with a red tile roof and original wood floors, windows and doors became a reality.

The deal closed, and I was the owner of a 1936 home. The day I moved in, I noticed that my neighbors came out to work in their gardens, if you call working pulling weeds without looking at what you are pulling. They trimmed one leaf at time from a branch and five minutes later they trimmed the next one. I waved at them, and they waved back. I saved the introductions for later, I needed to give instructions to the movers.

The next day, after having unpacked everything (but not putting away everything, I just wanted to not see more boxes), I was becoming anxious and decided to take Roland for a walk to the park and enjoy some fresh air. Packing stresses me, but unpacking almost gives me an anxiety attack. I cannot make a decision about where the best place for an item is, and I get worried that I will not have enough space for my stuff. I needed to get out of the house; I just took the house key and went to the park alone, leaving Roland to accompany Nolan. My cat was having a difficult time getting used to the new place, Nolan still was hiding under the bed most of the time. It took him a week to be back to being himself.

On my way back from the park, I met Frances who lives in the house on the corner next to mine. She said as soon as she saw me, "Hello dear, you must be the young lady that just moved in; are you the new owner?"

"Yes, I am. My name is Susana, but everybody calls me Susy." I replied with a big smile. I was happy to meet one of my new neighbors.

"I am Frances, I have lived here for forty years."

That day I spent close to an hour talking with Frances. She told me about herself and the rest of the neighbors. She gave me the highlights of the town and the neighborhood. She told me about the houses on our street, how they only had been sold once and that just like me she and her husband were the new kids on the block when they arrived, when they bought the house where Bonnie and Emma lived. She smiled when telling me she was pregnant with her first child when they arrived in the neighborhood. Then just around the time they decided to downsize, the owners of the little cottage on the corner moved and Frances and her husband went from the biggest house on the street to the smallest. There were so many memories made on this street that for them it seemed impossible to live somewhere else. When they bought their first house on Sea Foam Lane, all the inhabitants were couples with kids. Through the years the kids went off to college. Some of the originals died and others decided to move out of the city or closer to their families. She expressed how only women with their memories of begone years were left on this street and that she was happy somebody had arrived at Sea Foam Lane that was not retired. She likes the fact all the inhabitants are women but sometimes feels that having a man or two in the street would give her a feeling of safety. Frances told me who lives in each one of the houses, she just gave me facts. There was zero gossip about what she shared and I appreciated that. I could form my own opinion when I got to meet them.

In the next days after my arrival to the neighborhood, one by one, they stopped by to introduce themselves. Lesley brought me a fresh batch of homemade cookies and some baked treats for Roland. She told me how her schedule is driven around her grandchildren's activities; she is really happy to be part of their life on a daily basis versus just especial occasions. Even if she is exhausted by Friday, she will not have it any other way.

The Rogers sisters brought me an exquisite African violet; they are experts at growing African violets. They immediately invited me to go and see their backyard with mature orange, Meyer lemon and peach trees, and told me to not be shy and stop by to pick some fruit when I needed a fresh orange, lemon or peach. They also showed me the dozens of African violets that they have scattered through the house, I did not realize that there were so many varieties and colors; I was only familiar with purple and pink. The sisters explained to me that when they bought the house, they wanted extra space to have an area dedicated for their tutoring lessons. Today the room for the tutoring is a library and there are two beautiful distressed leather recliners and antique lamps around the room plus two baskets of yarn next to the chairs.

The most interesting introduction came from Miriam. It was a Saturday afternoon and I was watering the plants in the front. She was coming back from some event and after she parked her car, she crossed the street as if on a mission, her eyes focused on me.

"Hello there! You must be the new neighbor."

"Yes, I am." I said.

"I told Richard (the realtor), that the new owner needed to meet the age requirements. At least you meet the marital status requirement." Miriam was quick to mention.

I remember I was speechless. Did she just say, what I think she said? I do not have a poker face. I discovered Miriam did because after a few seconds of silence and my expression of disbelief, she started laughing.

"Susy, I am just joking, I am delighted that you are not close to sixty; we needed new blood, somebody with more energy in this place. If you are single, dating, divorced, married, it does not matter." Miriam assured me.

We talked for almost an hour, then her phone alarm went off, a reminder that she needed to get going to an outing with friends. I was relieved she was just joking; for a second, I was concerned she was going to be the nightmare neighbor.

Well, I made it to the grocery store, remembering those early days at my new home. It looks like the rush for last minute grocery shopping for Christmas has not started yet. The parking lot is not busier than any other Sunday. Hopefully I can find everything I need, otherwise I will need to go to another store, and I am not looking forward to going on a treasure hunt.

I AM GETTING BACK from the grocery store with the last ingredients for Christmas dinner when I turned into our little cul-de-sac. I see Frances taking her daily walk. She used to walk around the neighborhood and to the park, but everything changed during the summer when she had a hip replacement surgery, and she became more cautious. Then around October she started to walk to the park, but one afternoon on her way back she almost got run over by a distracted driver. Her alertness and a dog-walker screaming saved her from being hit. On the weekends I invite her to go walking when I take Roland to the park. She feels comfortable going with somebody else.

"Frances, would you like to go for a walk to the park?" I ask her as I am ready to close the garage door.

"Oh dear, you must be busy, I do not want to take your time."

"I am offering, I am taking Roland to play for a little and you can come."

"I will slow you down."

"Frances, nonsense. Let me put the groceries in the kitchen and get the leash on Roland's collar and we will be on our way, come in."

"Ok, let's go to the park, I will wait here in the garden."

My front door has a squeak. It is the alert system for my furry kids to know that I am back. I enter the house and Roland and Nolan are greeting me, their human is back!

"Ok, guys, let mommy put these bags in the kitchen." These two have the ability to get in front of you while carrying things. Now that the bags are on the kitchen island, I go to the laundry room to get Roland's leash. The laundry room has the aroma of lavender softener, I left towels washing and they are ready for the dryer. Roland is patiently waiting for me to finish putting the towels in the dryer and then get his leash. He sees that I reach for it and his exuberance grows ten-fold, his tail is moving so fast. Again, Nolan looks at me with disdain.

"Nolan, I wish I could take you to the park, but I do not think you would enjoy it, the park is no place for kitties, there are too many dogs."

Nolan meows back at me, at least it is what I think he does. He turns around and goes to the master bedroom which is his favorite place to nap at this hour of the day. The light hits the sliding door and there is certain warmth that Nolan enjoys. I know he is just putting on a show, he does not care. He will curl up in a space next to the left panel of the sliding door and stay there for hours.

"Roland, let's get out of the house this way." I close the back door.

"Frances we are ready." I tell Frances as we reach the front yard while Roland is wiggling his tail when he sees our walking companion waiting for us.

She is removing dead leaves and flowers from this massive geranium plant. She takes the little pile of trimmings and puts it in the green trash container.

"I should spend more time gardening, but lately with the short days I only can do it during the weekend, and I was sick with the flu for eight days after Thanksgiving." I say, trying to justify the pitiful state of my garden. Frances smiles at me understandingly and we head for the park.

It is amazing to see Roland taking the role of Frances' protector. When we encounter a walker, Roland gets closer to Frances. I think he feels Frances' uneasiness walking to the park. Our neighborhood is a collection of eclectic homes. You find Colonial, Craftsman, Mediterranean, old Spanish and few Art Deco houses. They were custom built as this is not a planned developmnent where most of the houses are similar. Regardless of the architectural style, the houses have something in common: their front yards are immaculate from roses to ground cover. Just beautiful curb appeal.

We arrive at our destination, a beautiful park that the decades have made more beautiful with mature palm, magnolia, pepper and pine trees. We walk by a fountain feeding a man-made creek while we proceed to our favorite spot, a hill in the middle of the park, perfect for tossing a tennis ball to Roland. He loves to run downhill and run up at full speed to give the ball back to me. He does not pay attention to the squirrels running from tree to tree or the pigeons coming closer to see if you have brought them some seeds or bread.

I enjoy so much seeing him running free. Finally, he gets tired. He keeps the ball and sits next to me, hyperventilating a bit with his tongue out, but happy to be outdoors. Frances has not said a word. She has been standing with her hands on her hips and with a look of melancholy while she inspects our surroundings. The park is the size of a block and at the end of the creek there is a small pond with ducks and turtles. On one of our first visits to the park Frances told me the turtles are there because somebody left a pair of them, and with the passing years they have multiplied. I always find it heartbreaking when people decide they do not want their pets anymore and just abandon them. At least these turtles were left in a nice location, but now there are thirty or forty. Soon the pond will not be big enough for all of them.

"I still remember," Frances starts talking, "when the park was full of kids almost every day. When we arrived in the neighborhood there were so many more children, plus more mothers were able to or chose to stay at home with their kids and they could bring them here on the weekdays. Now, we only see kids during the weekends. Back then I never thought that it was going to become one of the most sought-after places for weddings, quinceañeras and family portraits. I guess few areas are fairy-tale like." Frances pauses and breathes deeply, like she is trying to take in the aromas of all the different flowers at once.

"I wonder how this place will look in forty years?" I say, thinking aloud.

"Susy, most likely it will look the same. The trees will be bigger, you will be retired and maybe still enjoying this place, bringing your grandkids to play."

"Grandkids! Frances, I don't know if I am ready for children. I thought I was ready to get married, but I discovered my boyfriend was not ready to become my husband."

Frances puts her hand on my shoulder, "Susy, one day you will find the right man. Somebody who will not be able to imagine a life without you. Sometimes it takes time to find the right person. I do not know if you know, but Mark was not my first husband." Frances looks into my eyes and turns around to look at a family with a toddler on a tricycle.

"I did not know."

"I was so young when I married my first husband, who will remain nameless. I was a hopeless naïve teenager in love with romance. I was head over heels with a guy that was the perfect prince charming. I was not the only one convinced that he was the most eligible bachelor. My parents loved him, and my friends adored him. We got married. Shortly after the wedding, I discovered he was not prince charming; it was a mirage. He had created a perfect persona which started to crumble every day I spent with him, just leaving this total different man. The months living with him have been the most painful of my life. I would have divorced him earlier than I did, but my parents asked me to give him another chance. I was fortunate that few weeks later my father was told by a friend of the family that his son-in-law had a double life; he had a wife in North Dakota."

"Oh, Frances you must have been devastated."

"I was. For a while I did not want to trust another

man. I did not want to take any chances. One day I pushed myself to go out, I started dating. And without looking for the perfect man, Mark showed up in my life. Susy you just need to trust that there is somebody out there for you and that the day when you meet him is around the corner."

"I hope that day arrives soon, I do not want to run out of time. There are days that I think my biological clock is going to wind down."

"Oh, dear you still have years ahead of you to become a mother. You are not even forty."

"Yes, I may have still years to have kids, but I remember my mother raising my sisters and I and she used to get tired. Now I have seen my sisters, Diane and Maggie, with my nieces and nephews, and I just cannot imagine working and taking care of the kids."

"Maybe you do not work, and you just raise your kids."

"Well, I better find a wealthy husband."

"You need to find a caring man; the rest will just happen."

"I hope so. Growing up seeing my parents caring for each other and us was beautiful. I wish mom still was around with dad, it was not time for her to die."

"It is never time for a loved one to leave. How is your dad doing? I thought he was going to come to visit you for the holidays."

"He is doing great. He is actually on a tour of Costa Rica and Panama. After Thanksgiving I invited him to come and spend the holidays with me, but he told me he had a conflict in his schedule. A conflict that I totally understand. I do not think I told you but early in the year he had a medical crisis, and the doctors finally gave him the ok to travel. I still remember the day he received the good news. He called me and his voice sounded like a child who had just found out that Santa

Claus was getting him the present he had been waiting for. He sounded jovial; I could see him in my mind smiling as he was talking. One of the items on his bucket list was to go and see the Panama Canal. It is amazing how after facing death, priorities change. For his entire life he has put his family and the family business first. Now when he is reaching retirement age and after having a medical emergency, he has readjusted his priorities, which makes me happy. It is time for him to see the world and do the things he has been waiting to do for a long time, to check them off his bucket list."

"The days go by and if you are not paying attention, one day you find yourself looking at the mirror and wishing you had done more. Good for him. I wish my kids had invited me to stay with them during the holidays. But it was clear when I asked them that they did not have any intention of coming to visit or having me over for Christmas. My children quickly listed what their plans were – traveling to Yosemite, spending the holiday with the in-laws in Boston, and not affording to take time off from work. I did not bother to ask them if I could join them. I have three kids but it seems I am childless."

"That is too bad. Maybe next year you take one of those cruises you keep talking about."

"I do not know if I am ready to travel. After the hip surgery I don't feel too steady and don't like to be hustling through airports running from gate to gate."

"Frances, you are ready. Plus, you do not need to be running from gate to gate."

"I don't know, the last time I went to visit my eldest son, I only had fifty minutes to get to the gate and it felt like fifty seconds."

"Don't buy tickets with a small layover." Ventured Susy.

"I do not, my son bought then; I just didn't want to

deal with the computer, and I didn't want to ask him to change the tickets, I was happy I was going to see him and the grandchildren."

"Well next time you travel, I can help you book your trip."

"Oh, Susy you are too busy to be helping."

"I am never too busy for my favorite people in San Pedro."

"You are a doll."

"Frances are you ready to go back?"

"Yes, I am, let's go." She answers and starts to walk. Roland gets up and follows her.

We start to walk back home, taking a different path, covered by the canopies of the magnolia trees. It is beautiful at this time of the day with the light trickling through the leaves. It is a warm winter day. It started a little chilly, but in the last hours it just heated up. Soon we are back in our little street.

"Nice boy, I enjoy going for walks with you and your mommy." Frances says as she pets Roland's head. She opens the gate to her house and goes in. "Thank you, Susy for inviting me, it is nice to get out of the house. Besides the exercise, it helps me remember some of the moments that I spent there with Mark and the kids. Back then we used to walk to the park and sit on one of the benches overlooking the Harbor. We waited for the sunset and to see the full moon rise. Have you seen a moonrise lately?"

"No, I haven't. I don't remember when the last time I saw one was. But I saw the sunrise the other day on my way to work."

"Susy, seeing the sunrise while driving to work does not count. You cannot enjoy it. You need to start making some time to enjoy the little details in life. Work will always be there, but time will pass and one day you will be my age and you will be wishing you had done more." Frances opens the door to her cottage and smiles.

"I know Frances, I need to start taking more time for myself. Hey, I already started by not returning to work until January 3."

"That is a great way to start the year."

"I need to get home. The tamales are not going to prepare themselves."

"If you need any help, give me a call." Offers Frances.

"Thank you, Frances, I will let you know." I turn around as she waves goodbye.

I can't help but take a closer look at the mystery car left in front of my house. I am sure Emma and Bonnie may be looking through the sheer curtains of their house and if they are, they must be proud of me because I am peeking around. After studying the interior of the car, I am convinced that the car belongs to somebody moving to a different location or changing jobs. Or it could be somebody that just decided to take paperwork home. The car has leather seats in impeccable condition, the boxes in the back seat are filing boxes, the dry-cleaned shirts look almost new, plus there is a tie and pair of dressy black leather shoes on the floor of the back seat, confirming that the owner most likely is a man. There are some papers and envelopes on top of the boxes, but they are placed facing down. I cannot read to whom they are addressed. The only mess in the car is the fast-food wrappers and empty bottles of water and coconut water.

I inspect the exterior and the car is pristine, it almost seems that it had just been washed. I wonder if there is an online service that can tell me the name of the owner of the car by entering the license plate. It does not matter, what am I going to do with the information? Call a total stranger and tell him or her, "Hey, why did you leave your car in front of my house? Please come and get it before my neighbors call the tow truck."

I have things to do, I can't spend all day creating theories about why the car was abandoned. Roland is waiting patiently for me to finish with my investigation. "Ok this is enough," I tell Roland. "Let's get inside the house and see what your kitty brother is doing."

Wow, it is almost two o'clock and I have not had lunch. I cannot believe how fast the time has gone by. I will have a tuna sandwich. My recipe includes celery, Bermuda onion, mayo, fresh lemon juice, mustard, salt and pepper. Somedays I put capers in it, but today I do not feel like it. Roland is on his bed in the living room. Nolan is on my bed. He is such a prince; he opens his eyes and gives me a look when I walk in to change my shoes. He stretches and then curls up to go back to sleep. Sometimes I wonder if we just assign feelings to our pets, while for them there is such thing.

I do not want to eat my tuna sandwich in the dining room, I already cleaned in anticipation for Christmas. Most of the days I eat in the kitchen sitting on a bar stool at the little kitchen island. Today I am going to eat lunch in the living room and look out at the front yard, trying to do something different.

I just sit down to eat my sandwich when I notice an individual looking at the mystery car. I get up and move slowly, closer to the window to see if he is the owner. When I look closer, no, he is the mailman, a new mailman. I guess with the last-minute delivery of gifts for the holidays some postal employees are delivering packages outside their regular route, and on a Sunday. I am going to finish my sandwich outside in the back patio and just watch the birds and squirrels, then I think I will have a nap.

COUNTING SHEEP

*M*onday, December 24, 2018. Early morning.

It is 3:00 a.m. in the early morning and there is dense fog around the Palos Verdes Peninsula. The port is engulfed by it, only the top of the cranes is visible and the Vincent Thomas bridge towers over the fog. The fog has rolled in several miles inland and the Sea Foam cul-de-sac has a spooky look. As usual, the foghorn starts to make the echoing sounds alerting sailors of the dangerous weather conditions. San Pedro's longtime residents are used to the sound, they may be awakened by it, but they go back to sleep disregarding it. Susy still finds the sound unfamiliar and it always alters her sleeping pattern.

"Oh, what time is it? It is Sunday? Monday? Why did I set the alarm? Where is my phone?" I am more asleep than awake; I am trying to find the phone on the night-stand where I thought I left it. The alarm seems to have stopped, but I still want to find the phone and see what time is. If it is around 5:00 a.m., I will just get up and drink a cup of tea leisurely, make a fire and read. There is the sound again. Once again I was awakened by the foghorn and not my alarm. When am I going to get used to the sound? I turn on the night lamp, and Nolan who is sleeping by my feet, just rolls over when the light hits his face. He is an excellent foot warmer for the cold days. I get out of bed to look for the phone and finally I find it under one of the cushions that has fallen off the bed. It is only 3:08 a.m.!!!!! I need to get back to sleep, this is too early. I curl back up under the puffy comforter and close my eyes. I should be able to go back to sleep, everybody else in this town can.

It has been fifteen minutes since I tried to go back to sleep, I know because the foghorn just went off again. It didn't help either that yesterday's quick nap turned into a four-hour nap. Yep, pretty much I went from lunch to bed, then bed to dinner and back to bed. Now I find myself totally rested before 3:30 a.m. At this point I am awake and there is no point in lying here. I am not going to count sheep like I used to do when I could not fall asleep as a child. I am just going to get up and go to prepare a cup of tea, but it feels like a coffee type of morning. I am starting to look forward to just sitting in the living room and reading for a few hours. I put on the warmest bathrobe I have, and I take a throw blanket. I can hear Roland walking down the hallway. He sleeps in his bed in the living room but every morning when I get up, he makes his way to the bedroom to say good morning. Nolan in the other hand just stays on the bed sleeping or gives me a look that says "Human, how you dare to interrupt my sleep." I go to the kitchen and discover that I cannot see the back yard, visibility is only few feet. The ornamental garden solar lights illuminating the perimeter of the back patio have disappeared with the fog, only the first few lights are visible. I cannot even see the lawn chair and the little coffee table with the Talavera tiles. Most of the days, I drink tea, but I always keep a bag of ground French roast coffee just in case I wake up wanting something stronger or I have visitors that would like a cup. Roland is with me in the kitchen, waiting patiently for me to pour the cup of coffee. While the coffee is ready, I made my way in the dark to the dining room window, I want to see how the street looks with the fog at this hour. I pull aside the sheer curtain and see that the street has a spooky look, the trees look sinister. The fog is swirling at the end of the street, it is moving trying to find its way through the houses, trees and plants. This weather would have been perfect for Halloween. Instead we had Santa Ana wind conditions during Halloween, and it was a warm and dry day. I am wondering if Bonnie is also awake and peering through the curtains hoping for something to happen, and be the sole witness of any night activity in the cul-de-sac. In the darkness I make my way back to the kitchen to get my coffee.

"Roland, come on let's go to the living room and read for a while. We can worry about cooking later today." Roland wiggles his tale and follows me to the living room. I am debating if I should start a fire, but I do not want to deal with it this early. I set the coffee on the table. I look at the pile of books I have on the corner table, there is one I bought earlier in the year, but I haven't managed to get beyond the mid-point. When I try to read during weekdays, I am too tired, and I always fall asleep; my attempts to flip through a few pages is always futile. I have been tempted to just go to the final chapter and see how the story ends. It is not that I do not like the story, but I feel that I will never have the time to finish the book. I am giving myself until New Year's Eve to finish it, I should be able to since I don't have anything else to do besides taking care of my plants and exploring the town. I decide to grab a James Michener book that I have been reading for almost a year. I try to read at least twenty pages every weekend and I am really enjoying it, but even on the weekends I do not have too much time to spend hours reading. I like James Michener's works, but the number of pages in his books I find overwhelming. Anything over four hundred pages is overwhelming for me, and some of his books are over six hundred pages. I wrap the throw blanket around myself and I am ready to make the most of these early hours. Roland curls up in his bed and he will be sleeping a few more hours.

ALL OF A SUDDEN Roland is alert and I cannot hear what he is listening to. Then I hear the steps on the front porch and the doorbell rings. I spring up and take the first thing I see: the fire poker. Who can be ringing the doorbell at this hour? My phone vibrates and I see it is Miriam calling me. Roland gets up and goes to the door as if waiting for me to open it. I slowly go back to the kitchen while I answer Miriam's call.

"Hello, Miriam I think somebody is by my door." I say as quietly as I can.

"Yes, there is somebody. It's me." What could Miriam want at this hour and why she did not call first? I turn the entrance light on, deactivate the alarm and open the door. Roland is wagging his tail by my side and waiting eagerly to great our early visitor.

"Good morning, Miriam! This visit at 5:30 a.m. is quite a surprise. What is going on?" I ask as I let her in. She looks awake, full of energy. She is wearing boots, black jeans, a nice camel jacket and a black knitted hat –

a stylish and well-coordinated outfit for 5:30 am. Where does this woman get all her energy? She walks in and I show her to the living room.

"I woke up about an hour ago with the sound of the foghorn, plus with the passing of years I have lost the ability to sleep the whole night, not that I ever was able to sleep from sundown to sunrise. Now I may wake up in the middle of the night and then I just cannot go back to sleep. After going through some mail and looking at all-inclusive vacation catalogs, I decided to come out to check if the newspaper had been delivered and I saw the light in your living room was on, and I thought to check if you were awake. I saw you reading and well, that is when I knocked the door. Sorry if I scared you, I should have called you or texted you first."

"Yes, Miriam. You scared me a little, the only reason I was not too scared was because Roland did not bark." Miriam smiles and points at the fire poker leaning against the wall.

"I think you were more than a little scared. Sorry, about the morning intrusion."

"It's ok, I woke up at three with the foghorn and I tried to go back to sleep without success. Then I decided to catch-up on my reading."

"Well Susy, would you like to join a photography expedition to the port of Los Angeles for a winter sunrise?" I can't help but look at Miriam with disbelief, I never have seen fog this thick and she expects to take pictures of the sunrise.

"I don't know if you will be able to take any pictures of the sunrise due to the lack of visibility, I can't see your house from here."

"Susy, if you come along, you may be in for a surprise. What do you say? Let's go explore San Pedro before sunrise. We could go for an early breakfast after the photo shooting adventure."

"I need to take Roland out around seven, I do not know if I can be out that long." I say to Miriam.

"Susy, just bring him along. I know the perfect place for breakfast, and the owner loves dogs. What do you think Roland, should your mom take you out for a drive around town?" She is petting Roland between the ears, and he is loving it.

"Ok, Miriam, I guess we will go with you. What do I have to lose? This book will still be here when I come back, and I have the feeling this is not the first time you have done one of these early morning photography expeditions."

"That's the spirit. See you in ten minutes outside my garage. Bring some coffee." Miriam gets up and lets herself out. I walk to the kitchen to get ready one more cup of coffee.

"Roland, I guess we will have a tour of the town before sunrise." I pet him as I pass by to go to the laundry room and get an old blanket that I have for when I take long car trips with the dog. I do not want him scratching Miriam's back seat. I go to the bedroom to change. Nolan is on the bed in the same spot as when I left him two hours ago. I admire the furball's ability to sleep. I wish I could curl-up like him and just drop off to sleep in an instant.

Carefully and trying not to make too much noise, I close the front door and cross the street to Miriam's house. She already has taken her car out of the garage. I get Roland in the back seat, and he immediately lays down on his blanket. I get in tand we are ready to go.

We get to the entrance of our little street, and it is like we are facing a white gray curtain. The visibility is limited, at the most three or four feet. You cannot see the cars parked on the street, nor the sidewalk. The fog is slowly rolling, it looks like giant white and gray cotton-candy balls rolling down the street. I start to wonder if this is such a great idea. I take a deep breath and try to relax my head against the seat. Roland can feel my uneasiness and makes a small noise. I turn around and reach to try to pet him to show that I am ok.

"Ok, lets got to the left and go to the hill. The view from there is amazing if the fog is low in the harbor. The lights of the cranes and the contrast with the fog is pretty good." Miriam says and then puts the left blinker on and drives like there is no fog in the street. It is interesting to see the town at this hour. I have driven to work early in the morning, but always taking the same route. I have never been at this hour of the day and time of the year driving around town, exploring the different neighborhoods that San Pedro has. Miriam on other hand seems like she has been researching the best spots to take pictures under these weather conditions. She turns the radio on to a classical music station and she has a little smile on her face, almost a look of excitement. The anticipation is visible. I remain silent as we drive through the streets, engulfed in the thick fog. I am wondering how many people are awake because of the foghorn. Between stops and sips of our coffees we reach a hill. Miriam is driving slowly, we pass by an old Victorian mansion with two lanterns in the front of the property, one of them is flickering and the other seems dimmed with the swirling fog. The image reminds me of black and white horror movies- if the street had cobblestones, it would be perfect. We keep going uphill for two more blocks; the fog it is getting lighter and suddenly we are out of it. Miriam is looking for a place to park. The street seems pretty busy with cars parked on it. This is a neighborhood with apartment buildings, most of them built with Old Spanish touches: red cement pathways taking you to wooden doors with wrought iron accents, window frames painted in dark green, white stucco and red tile roofs.

"Aha, it's our lucky day, we will not need to walk too far to get to one of my favorite spots." Miriam says. Quickly she parallel parks like a pro, turns off the motor, takes a sip of her coffee, and opens the trunk to retrieve her camera and gear. I get out of the car and move the passenger seat to take Roland out.

"Miriam, would you like me to take your coffee or help you with your gear?" I offer as I take my cup. Being awake since three and the chill in the air are starting to make me want to go back to bed. Roland is excited, definitely he is embracing this early adventure. His tail is wagging nonstop.

"Thank you, I got this, and I am done with my coffee." Miriam responds and she takes her bag and tripod out of the trunk before even I could finish my sentence.

"Roland, don't get any ideas I will be getting up this early to take you exploring every day." I tell my dog that is just ecstatic.

"Susy you may want to change your routine now and then. It is amazing the change in the energy of your day when you do something different." Miriam says as we walk to the corner and cross diagonally to the other side of the street. I turn around and I see the fog down the street, everything is calm, quiet. I see three guys in the next block walking toward us. Roland becomes alert and gets closer to me. For the second time, I am wondering if this was a good idea after all. I think Miriam just chuckled. One of the guys runs toward us, I hold Roland's leash and take a deep breath.

"Hello sweetie!" Miriam says, greeting the individual wearing a beanie knit hat and a denim jacket.

"Hey girl, we haven't seen you in a while. Did you get lost? You missed some awesome November skies." He says as he takes away the tripod from Miriam.

"I was out of the country for a few days and then I didn't feel like getting out of the house early. But today I couldn't miss the chance to see if the fog was going to put on a show. Rob this is my friend Susy."

"Hello, I think I saw you in Miriam's summer BBQ. Nice to meet you, Susy. Hey buddy." Rob nods at me as he pets Roland, who enjoys the extra attention.

"Hi Rob." I do not remember seeing him before, but I remember going to Miriam's summer BBQ. It was the event of the year on our street.

"The twins always move so slow." Miriam says as the other two guys meet us in the middle of the block.

"Good morning, ladies." Both guys say in unison. They are identical twins, and they are dressed identically but one has long hair and the other short.

"Susy, these are the Walters brothers, Gregory and Joshua." Rob says.

"Along with Rob, they are the three musketeers of sunrise and sunset photography." Miriam adds.

"Hello Susy, call me Greg."

I smile and shake his hand. I am making a mental note that Greg is the one with the short hair.

"Susy, I go by Josh. Why have we not seen you before? Miriam, have you been keeping away from us your beautiful friends?" Josh says as he gives an inquisitive look to Miriam.

"Yes, I have because I know you, and I don't want you breaking anyone's hearts. You are Don Juan De-Marco or should I say Don Josh De San Pedro!" Everybody laughs and Rob pushes Josh while he shakes his head. Josh shrugs his shoulders.

"Ouch that hurt, Miriam. Susy, do not believe anything that you hear about me." Josh puts his hands in his heart and then he winks at me.

"I am not like him, even if I look like him." Greg says and also winks at me. I just keep smiling.

"Now that we are done with all the pleasantries, let's take some pictures." Miriam says as she unpacks her camera. Rob opens her tripod and then just stands back as Miriam starts setting up the camera. The twins are getting their equipment ready, one taking care of the tripod while the other takes two cameras out of a backpack. I look around and there is nobody on the street.

The view from here is spectacular: to my left is the Vincent Thomas bridge to Terminal Island, in front of me are the cranes, and in the distance are the mountains. To the right, a bit of the coastline can be seen where the fog ends. It seems like the fog knows exactly where the port is because it has covered it uniformly, only the tops of the cranes are visible.

"It is a pretty sight, isn't it?" Rob asks as he gets closer to me and pets Roland.

"It is. Until this moment I didn't have any idea this place existed. Miriam had to twist my arm to get me out of the house." I reply.

"Well, I am happy she did. I thought everybody on her street was her age."

"I am the only one under sixty at Sea Foam Lane. Are you not taking pictures?"

"Yes, I am. Whatever I can take with this." Rob pulls out his smartphone from the pocket of his worn-out jeans. "No fancy cameras and lenses for me. How about you?"

"I have a camera that I bought to take pictures when I went to a tropical beach for vacation. By the end of the vacation, I had taken most of my pictures using the phone. The camera has not seen the light of the day in months. I like photography but I haven't taken the time to go and take pictures." I say. I do not tell him that there is a second reason why I haven't taken the camera out of the closet- I don't want to go through the pictures in the memory card. The vacation to the tropical island was with my "Ex" and he is in most of the pictures. It has been almost eighteen months since we parted ways. While I am over him, I do not want to see his face in the pictures I need to delete. I should have deleted them last year just after breaking up with him, but instead I was crying and using all the tissues I had in the house.

The minutes go by and Rob and I are taking in the view, appreciating the peacefulness of this quiet early morning. The silence is interrupted by the occasional sound of the foghorn. We are content looking at the fog rolling inland. It is nice to be with somebody in comfortable silence; there is no need to be making conversation when enjoying a beautiful morning. Miriam and the Walters twins are adjusting the settings on their cameras, taking shots every few minutes. Rob takes out his phone and takes a picture. He shows it to me and then deletes it. It was ok but nothing worth keeping.

"I cannot capture the beauty of this moment. Sometimes there are memories that are vivid in your mind more than what your photo can capture, and today is one of those moments." Rob says as he puts the phone back in his pocket.

"Boys, what do you say we go by the Lookout Point Park, take some shots from there and then go and get breakfast." Miriam says as she removes the camera from the tripod.

"Now you are talking, girl!" Josh exclaims and puts one of the cameras in the backpack.

"Breakfast sounds good." Rob rubs his belly in anticipation.

"Rob likes to eat." Josh says.

"Josh also likes to eat but he never talks about food. He just devours anything that gets in front of him when he is hungry." Rob replies as he walks towards the car.

"Guys, see you at the next stop. Susy let's get out of

here. You will love the spot and I believe you are going to see one of the most spectacular sunrises of the year." Says Miriam. I follow her to the car, and we are on our way to this place that she is claiming to be breathtaking.

"WHAT DO YOU THINK SUSY? Would you do this again?" Rob asks. We have been looking at the changing view: at the intensity of the sky colors stealing the spotlight from the city lights, to the mountains appearing from the darkness dwarfing the cranes in the port. The splendor of the new day approaches.

"I think this is beautiful. Yes, I will do this again. I may just one day wake up early and come here and wait for the sunrise." I replied without moving my head. I do not want to miss the moment when the sun reveals itself over the mountains.

The minutes have gone by, and the sunrise is almost over. To my surprise a few more avid photographers showed up to this spot. By the way they are greeting Miriam and the twins it seems everybody knows everybody. Just like Miriam said, it was spectacular. The sky went from dark purple to orange hues. There were a few clouds making it even more breathtaking as they changed from red-orange to pink tones. As the sun rose, the contour of the mountains was defined by the light and the contrast with the sky. Adding to the spectacle was the fog hovering over the port. I do not remember the last time I saw a sunrise as dramatic as this. It was just yesterday that I was telling Frances I have seen sunrises on my way to work, but I never have seen a sunrise like this in all the years I have lived in Los Angeles. I am happy I came with Miriam.

"Hey guys, before going to breakfast let's stop by the

Korean Friendship Bell and take some pictures of the moon, it was full two days ago." Greg recommends.

"Let's do it." Miriam says.

"Susy do not believe Miriam or the twins when they say it is their last shot because there is always something else they want to photograph, or they swear the light has changed and it is perfect. They will find different reasons not to turn off the camera." Rob says as he shrugs his shoulders and turns around to get into the car with Josh and Greg.

"I hope this will be the last stop because I am getting hungry. C'mon Roland let's go." I say as we get into the car only to get out of it within a minute. I had driven more than once through this area and had seen the Asian temple-like structure on the hilltop, but never stopped to explore it.

Greg was right, the view of the almost full moon over the ocean and the palm trees on Paseo Del Mar make a nice composition. It is a clear day now that the fog was burnt off from this side of the peninsula. You can see the terrain details of Santa Catalina Island even if it is twenty-six miles away. Visiting Santa Catalina Island has been on my things to do in Los Angeles list since my summer internship. Rob and I walk around looking at the concrete pads where during WWII coastal artillery guns were located. I let Roland explore a little. If I had known I would have brought his tennis ball since there is a hill where I can see him running up and down fetching it.

"Susy, a few more shots and we will go and get breakfast at the best diner in town." Miriam says as she is looking through the viewfinder and making adjustments to capture the moon over the ocean, with the coastline as a backdrop. "Just, one more." Miriam reassures me as she takes her camera and tripod and moves few feet away to take the perfect shot. Rob looks at me, winks and says in a hushed tone "I told you."

"Susy, are you ready for breakfast?" Josh puts the lens caps on, removes the camera neck strap and at last his camera goes into the backpack. I realize he has been taking pictures of the streets, cars, trees and buildings more than of the sunrise and moon.

"Yes, I am ready for breakfast. Waking up so early has built quite an appetite. I need a cup of coffee. Do you guys do this often?" I ask.

"Not as often as we wish. Work gets is the way. But when there is an opportunity, we go out in search for that shot that will make our day." Says Josh.

"Have you known Miriam for a long time? Where did you meet her?" I inquire further. I am curious how they met my jovial neighbor.

"Maybe for three years. We met her in a gallery in the old part of town. After talking with her for a while we invited her to join us in for a sunrise photo shoot; now she is part of the group of local photography aficionados that get together to take pictures of different events and things around town.

"Like a photography club?" I ask.

"We are not that organized. We are just a spontaneous bunch that enjoy photography. Some like us are amateur photographers, while others just like to come along to enjoy the scenery and chat, go to galleries, or meet for an impromptu social hour at one of the downtown bars." Josh explains.

"I see." I guess I need to get out of the house and go check downtown one of these weekends.

"How about you, when did you meet Miriam?" Josh asks.

"I met her when I became her neighbor, almost a year and a half ago."

"She is a great lady and so fun to be around." Josh offers.

"Yes, I am discovering that. I should try to spend more time with her. Today the foghorn woke me up around three and I ended up reading because couldn't fall asleep. By five Miriam was at my door convincing me to join her in her early morning adventure." Josh smiles as he shakes his head.

"What?" I ask him.

"It's funny, I never thought that somebody young would live on that street. I thought everybody was re-tired. Now, I will try to visit Miriam more often and maybe I'll get to see you." He smiles and turns away to see the pristine coastline and the moon getting lost in the horizon. I just remain silent and enjoy the moment.

"Breakfast time! I am ready for some bacon and eggs!" Greg says excitedly. He has been quiet most of the morning.

"Let's do it!" Rob replies.

We start to walk to the cars, and I am happy we are going to breakfast because I am hungry, and bacon is sounding pretty good right know.

On Paseo del Mar people are out and about now that the sun is up. I am going to make sure that on weekends I take one of my runs here. It will be great to look at the ocean, feel the breeze on my face and enjoy the salt air. I also can bring Roland to the Point Fermin Park with unobstructed views of Santa Catalina Island.

We turn right on a street with a steep incline, making our way up the hill with Roland curl up in the back seat. I am observing the different houses, streets, trees and peacocks!!! Yes, there is a group of peacocks crossing the street.

"Peacocks?" I exclaim as Miriam slows down to let them cross. Definitely this morning has been full of surprises: amazing harbor views, a wonderful sunrise, meeting three of Miriam's friends, and now peacocks.

"Oh yes, there are a lot of peacocks in this section of town. It is quite a spectacle when they walk around displaying their feathers. There are even street signs asking you to slow down and watch out for peacocks crossing the street. Our diner is just a few blocks away." Miriam points out the sign on the next corner showing a peacock crossing the street.

I am a little embarrassed that I thought I had explored the town. In the last two hours I have realized my exploration was cursory at best- I may know our little area a few blocks around the cul-de-sac. The day I made the offer for the house I explored the main street and some of the area, but just enough to see if I saw something I did not like. I have not really gone out and just wandered the different neighborhoods. I should follow Miriam's recommendation and do something different. Maybe once per month I should explore, get out of the weekend routine of doing laundry, going shopping, running errands, trying to read, cooking a few lunches and meals for the week and then getting to Sunday night exhausted and collapsing in bed tired, just for Monday to start all over again. I need to make time for things like this.

"How did the peacocks get here?" I ask, hoping Miriam has the answer. It will save me some online research.

"The story is that some of the wealthy habitants in the early 1900's brought them to have them in their mansions. But with time the birds escaped or were left behind when their owners went back to their other estates. Now you get to see them wandering some of the older neighborhoods in Los Angeles, like in Pasadena, Altadena, and Arcadia." As I thought, Miriam had the answer on the tip of her tongue.

We are slowing down and we are parking across from the diner. There is an OPEN neon sign with green letters in one of the windows. An old tin sign with fading letters in blue, is hanging above the door, it only says *Angelo's.*

"Here we are, Angelo's Diner, a landmark in the South Bay. It has been here since the '60s. Best place in town for breakfast and the best South Bay sandwiches." Miriam says as she opens the door and gets out of the car. The guys are already sitting at a table in the patio of the little dinner. The garden has citrus trees and an avocado tree. There are red cannas and pink hibiscus plants flowering, and a fountain in one corner. There are only four tables, making it a really cozy garden; there are more tables inside, but with a mild winter morning why not enjoy the outdoors, plus we have Roland. The menus are already on the table.

"What took you so long?" Josh asks as we enter the patio. He gets up to pull out the chair for Miriam. Rob stands up and quickly pulls out my chair.

"Wow Rob, this is the first time I have seen you being a gentleman!" Josh exclaims as both sit down.

"Maybe because you never pay attention to anything besides your phone." Rob is quick to reply as everybody chuckles.

"Good morning, my name is Ellie! Do you have any questions about the menu? Are you ready to order?" The waitress asks as she puts down two pots of coffee on the next table. We reply in unison, "We are ready." She takes our order and pours us coffee. I do not know why, but it seems the coffee from restaurants always has a better aroma than any pot I prepare at home. She returns with the orange juices that the twins asked for and she brings two dog cookies for Roland.

"Susy, where are you from? Because I don't remember seeing you around." Greg asks. This is the first time he is talking to me. He exchanged words with Miriam, but he didn't speak to me besides the morning greetings. His brother, Josh, is a chatterbox. Greg seems more reserved, or maybe he is not a morning person.

"I am originally from Wisconsin. In my last year in college, I got an internship in a local company which turned into a job offer. Before moving to San Pedro, I rented in El Segundo, Lawndale and Hermosa, trying to stay close to work and explore different neighborhoods."

"If you had not missed Miriam's BBQ, you may have met Susy there." Rob informs Greg.

"Hey, it was grandma's 75th birthday. We couldn't miss her birthday celebration; it was the biggest family reunion in years." Josh defends their absence from Miriam's party of the year.

"*You* went to the BBQ. Can you explain how you did not meet her there?" Greg accuses Rob. This is the most lively I have seen Greg since I met him on the hill.

"Maybe because he was there only five minutes." Miriam interjects.

"Hey, at least I showed up, not like other people I know. Miriam, you know I wanted to stay longer but Mrs. Walters was not going to be happy if I missed her 75th bash. I did not want to be banished from any future Walters' clan gatherings." Claims Rob.

"I guess I will forgive the three of you. But I expect to see you at my next party, and I will not accept any excuses." Miriam says smiling.

"We will be there, promise." Josh replies for the three of them.

"Susy, what do you do in your spare time? Greg asks. I am surprised- a second question from Greg.

"Well, I do not have too much spare time these days, but when I have, I like to read and work in the garden."

"Do you like any outdoor activities besides gardening? Rob asks.

"I enjoy going to the park to walk Roland or to go running. How about you guys?" I ask all of them. I do not want this breakfast to turn into an interrogation about my life.

"Greg and I like surfing and snowboarding when there is enough snow in the mountains, and we are always open for a pickup basketball game." Josh is quick to add.

"I do some surfing. But my favorite activity by far is hiking. Whenever I have the chance to get out of town I do, and go to hike trails as far as the central coast, usually making a weekend road trip out of it." Rob interjects.

I find Rob attractive. Grey eyes, thick eyebrows, olive complexion and a beautiful smile. He is not a handsome pretty-boy type but an attractive man. The twins are more handsome but have the pretty-boy look.

"Well, *my* preferred outdoor activity is to have a pitcher of my favorite drink, mint julep, under an umbrella while sunbathing in the backyard." Miriam says.

"That's my girl." Josh exclaims.

"I thought your favorite drink was a margarita." Rob asks surprised.

"Well, my dear Rob, my favorite drink depends on the season and who is paying." Miriam answers as she winks her eye and raises her coffee as if she is going to toast. We just laugh. A mature and fit man with an apron is coming toward us with a wine glass and orange juice.

"Good morning. I was told my favorite customer is here."

"Good morning, Angelo! Thank you. Stop spoiling me. How do you know mimosas are my favorite?" Miriam says as she greets Angelo with a flirty smile and takes from his hand the wine glass with a generous mimosa. As Miriam and Angelo are exchanging pleasantries, I look at the twins and Rob and we just smile thinking about what she just told us a second ago. I guess a complementary mimosa is her drink of choice at the moment.

"Hey Angelo! I am going to tell Nana that she is not your favorite." Josh says as he shakes his head with an expression of disappointment.

"Yeah Angelo, the other day I was here with my auntie Lucy, and you told her the same." Rob chimes in.

"Oh boys, all of them are my favorites in their own special way. But why should I say, you are one of my favorites, if *"you are my favorite"* sounds better to the lady that is present at the moment. You guys need to learn how to make a woman feel unique." Angelo slaps Rob on the head.

"Well said Angelo. You, young man, have learned something today. Thank you for the mimosa." Miriam says as she raises her glass towards Angelo. She flickers her eyelashes and then proceeds to take a delicate sip from the glass.

"You are welcome my dear. And who do we have here? I never have seen this lovely young lady before."

"I am Susy, Miriam's neighbor."

"And friend." Miriam adds quickly.

"Susy, I hope you like our food, and we get to see you again." Says Angelo.

"I am sure I will be back. They have been talking about your place for the last few hours."

"And we will be waiting to serve you the best breakfast in town. And talking about breakfast, I need to check on yours."

"Yes, Angelo we are ravenous." Josh says as he puts his hand on his belly to emphasize how hungry he is.

"You always are, Joshy!" Angelo turns around and goes back in.

"Josh, you guys are twins but have different color eyes!" Before Josh responds to Angelo's comment. I exclaim when I notice that his eyes are a honey color while Greg's are green.

"We both wear contacts and to avoid mixing them up we decided one of us should wear tinted contacts. Plus it is easier to find them if you drop them when trying to get them on." Greg replies.

"Joshy who wears the tinted contacts?" Rob asks trying to annoy Josh.

"You already know Robby. Don't call me Joshy. Only my Nana and few special people get away with calling me Joshy. One day Susy may get away with calling me Joshy."

I just smile, while Rob and Greg roll their eyes at Josh's comment. I excuse myself to go to the restroom.

To my delight I find my breakfast on the table waiting for me when I return. Rob gets up right away to pull my chair out for me. As I sit, Angelo is coming to our table with a second mimosa in hand.

"Is everything as you expected? This is for you Susy, on the house to celebrate your first visit to our diner." Angelo says as he puts the mimosa in front of my plate, while raising his hand to signal Josh, Greg and Rob not to ask him about their free mimosas.

"If you rascals don't stop complaining. I will not share with you…" Angelo takes out of his apron pocket a small bottle of hot sauce.

"We are quiet." Rob says as Josh and Greg shake their heads in agreement.

"Bon appétit!" Angelo puts the bottle with the hot sauce closer to their plates and turns around to go back to the kitchen.

"Hey! Angelo, you're the man! Thank you, Angelo! Thanks, this is our lucky day." Rob, Greg and Josh are so excited about the small bottle of sauce. They have turned into little kids with the unexpected delivery from Angelo.

"Susy, Angelo prepares this hot sauce using a family recipe that has been passed down through the generations. The story goes that the family of his great-great-grandmother was from Spain. Most of Angelo's family is from Italy. The recipe has been prepared through the generations using chiles brought to Spain by the first explorers that returned to Spain from America. Angelo remembers seeing his grandmother and then his mother planting the seeds, watering the plants and patiently waiting to harvest the chiles to prepare the hot sauce. Because Angelo follows the family recipe and only uses the chiles from those seeds, he only produces a small batch of the sauce and only shares it with his most loyal customers, and only when he feels like sharing it, just like his father Angelo Sr. did when he opened this place in the '60s. This may be one of the best kept secrets in San Pedro. These three hungry boys definitely are loyal customers. Let's eat." Miriam recounts the wonderful story behind the coveted hot sauce bottle.

ALL OF A SUDDEN there is silence. Everybody is concentrating on eating. I have to admit, the omelet with vegetables and the breakfast potatoes are delicious. The fresh sourdough bread is really good. I am glad I only got one slice because if there were more slices, I would eat them all. In just few minutes we have devoured the food. Everybody looks relaxed and satisfied. The waitress brings the check and the guys put their share on the tray. Miriam adds some bills to cover our share and counts all the money, making sure there is enough left for the tip.

"Ok, let's go." Miriam says as she gets up and takes the tray with the money to Angelo. He takes it from her hand and puts it in his apron pocket. He embraces Miriam in a warm hug and kisses her on the cheeks.

"Hey, why do we not get a hug?" Josh asks.

"Because you guys are too ugly!" Angelo replies.

Everybody laughs and we walk through the dining room where other customers are sitting enjoying breakfast and coffee.

"Happy we got to see you, Miriam! Nice meeting you Susy!" Greg says as he hugs Miriam and then waves at me. He definitely is the quiet twin. Identical twins with different personalities.

"I hope to see you soon you too, and Merry Christmas." Josh says goodbye and crosses the street to the car.

"Merry Christmas Miriam!" Rob gives a big hug to Miriam.

"It was nice seeing you boys. Merry Christmas to you and your families. Let's get together after the New Year." Miriam waves and walks towards the car. Rob is standing next to me and pulls out his phone.

"I enjoyed talking with you this morning. It was an unexpected surprise to meet you. I am happy the foghorn woke you up. Susy, would you like to go hiking on one of the local trails sometime later in the week or maybe for a cup of coffee or both?" Inquires Rob.

"It was nice meeting you too, and the twins also. Sure, I have the week off." I say, a little surprised about his invitation, but why not to go out and do something different this week. After all, this morning was not planned and had turned out to be a wonderful time.

"Great, then can I get your phone number?" Rob looks into my eyes, and I feel goosebumps.

"Rob what is taking you so long. We are going to leave you behind!" Josh shouts across the street. I give him my phone, he smiles and pets Roland. "Thank you, see you soon Susy!" He turns around and runs to the car.

"Come on Roland, it looks like mommy got a date."

IT IS ALMOST nine and we are getting back to our little cul-de-sac. The fog has dissipated. There are few cars on the streets; after all today is Christmas Eve. While the day started way too early, it was a great outing. I discovered areas of San Pedro that I never even have driven by. On several occasions Miriam has invited me to join her for some of her activities, but work got in the way, and I couldn't accept. It the future I may reorganize my work schedule to join Miriam on one of her outings; there is guaranteed fun with her. I hope when I am her age I have the same zest for life as she does.

We pull behind the yellow car that is in front of my place. To my surprise there is a big poinsettia plant in a beautiful red and green pot waiting for me on the other side of the picket fence.

"What is that?" I exclaim as I look at the unexpected delivery.

"It is a poinsettia my dear."

"I know that Miriam, but I was not expecting any deliveries."

"Then you have a secret Santa!" Miriam says with a tone of excitement.

I get out of the car without even taking Roland from the back seat. I go straight to the plant to try to find a note on it. Miriam is following me and stands next to me waiting to know who the sender is. I find a little golden envelop and try to open it carefully. I tend to open gifts and greeting cards with care even if it takes forever.

"Come on Susy just tear it open, either way it's going to end up in the recycle bin." I give a look to Miriam who is anxiously waiting for me and do just what she tells me. I tear open the envelop and inside there is a piece of paper folded carefully many times. As I unfold the ivory sheet of paper, I see familiar handwriting. I feel chills going through my body. I read it in silence while Miriam is waiting for me to say something.

"Dear Susy, Merry Christmas, wishing I were with you. The last months I have realized how much I miss you. I believe our breakup was a mistake. If I could ask for one wish during this holiday season, it will be to get a second change. Love Taylor"

I hand over the note to Miriam and put my face in my hands.

"Why does he do this? Why does he intrude into my holidays?"

"Who is Taylor?" Miriam asks after reading the note.

"My ex, the one that I spent almost four years with, the one that ran away when I asked what the future of our relationship was. Because I wanted to move to the next phase, marriage. He just wanted to move in together without additional attachments. I spent the second half of last year forgetting about him, healing slowly the open wounds remaining. After breaking up with him I discovered he had been seeing somebody else while we were still dating. One of my friends that is active in social media told me that he had seen them together hugging and kissing at a summer pool party in a fancy hotel in Palm Springs. It was not a weekend fling because when my friend went searching in social media for postings tagged to the hotel; he found a posting of Taylor and his date. Then looking at her profile he discovered more pictures of them, celebrating birthdays, romantic dinners, weekend trips and more. It's funny, he didn't like taking photos with me to post in social media, but there he was, all smiles and holding her in his arms."

I never had told the whole story about my breakup to my neighbors. Frances knew a little, but not the cheating part. While there is no point in hiding my past from the people I share my present, I did not want to spend any time talking about Taylor with them nor recounting his dishonesty.

"Susy, I would not give too much importance if he showed up now and during the holidays. You should be happy that the guy is alone and most likely was dumped or finally woke up to the realization that you loved him and really wanted a life together. Forget him. Do not even bother to open the door if he shows up. He had his chance. It is none of my business, but you are my friend and I do not want to see you sad or hurt by somebody who is not worth it." Miriam stops talking and hands over the piece of paper, which I crumble into a small ball, and go to toss it in the trash bin. I pick up the flowers to put them in the trash.

"Wait Susy, if you do not want those flowers don't put them in the trash. If you don't mind, I will take them. I am visiting my friend Lily at lunch. She has been confined to her house for a few days due to a surgery and I can give the poinsettias to her. She loves them. This unwanted gift can provide somebody else joy and the flowers will not die in a trash bin. They may even flower next year under Lily's care." Miriam takes away the heavy plant and puts it on the sidewalk.

"You are right, the plant can make somebody else happy." I see that Roland is sitting in the back seat waiting to be taken out of his confinement.

"Roland, come out boy, let's get you out."

"If it is ok with you, I will leave the plant here, I will take it when I am ready to leave." Offers Miriam.

"Sure."

"Let's do this again. It was fun to have you and Roland riding along." She says as she is getting ready to get in her car.

"Yes, it was fun. Thank you for showing me that there is more to see than the boring route I take when I get the freeway every day!"

Miriam gets in her car. I close the gate. Miriam is right, I cannot give importance to some holiday desperate action of Taylor. If he is alone for the holidays there is a reason for it, karma.

COOKING WITH MEMORIES

*A*fter returning from this morning's excursion time flew by – fed the fur babies, took a shower, talked with some of the relatives, had a call with dad, and then it was time for lunch. I had spaghetti, with Italian hot sausage (made by the local butcher), grilled red bell peppers, caramelized onions and sautéed garlic. I was really hungry; it seems like my body consumed the delicious breakfast from Angelo's quickly and by noon I was ravenous.

I had a second surprise this morning; a voicemail from my friend Cindy: "Susy, I hope you are not upset that I gave your new address to Taylor. He seemed so sad and pleaded with me non-stop to give him your address. He said he had a GIFT for you!" I love Cindy but sometimes her common sense is zero, and she still believes in fairy tales. She forgot all the tears I cried in her apartment after breaking up with Taylor, and the emotional turmoil when our friend, Scott, told me he had seen Taylor in Palm Springs with his new girlfriend. It turned out to be an old girlfriend. I texted Cindy to forget it, but I made it clear this should be the last time she shares my personal information (address, phone number and e-mail). She cannot be giving out other people's info like candy on Halloween. It doesn't matter if they tell her that they need to find me because I just inherited millions from a lost relative.

Now that lunch it is out of the way, it is time to start preparing the dishes for tomorrow's feast. Today I am cooking the tamales and the chicken for the green pozole. Tomorrow I will finish the pozole. I will not be preparing dessert because Lesley graciously offered to prepare a yule log cake and gingerbread cookies. While she is going to have dinner with her family at one of her kids' houses, she insisted on bringing dessert for the Sea Foam Lane Christmas dinner.

Emma and Bonnie will be sharing a batch of eggnog; Emma is in charge of preparing it based on their family recipe. I will have a sip as a courtesy since I never have been a fan of eggnog. Everybody in my family likes to drink the stuff, but I don't like milk, so maybe that is the reason for my distaste, or the heavy cream in it. I am from Wisconsin - one of the states known for their cheese production, and I do not eat cheese nor drink milk but I eat ice cream. My sisters never have understood my distaste for cheese and milk but my love for ice cream.

Frances offered to buy firewood. I was envisioning a bundle or two, or a few fire logs. To my surprise last Saturday morning the doorbell rang and Peter, Frances' gardener, was standing on the porch asking me where I wanted the firewood. I said here, in the living room. He smiled and said as he pointed to his truck and then back to my living room, "Miss Susy, all that, in there?" The back of his pick-up truck was overloaded with firewood. He reassured me all the firewood was for me and that Frances already had enough to last her a year. I asked Peter to stack it next to the back door. I will take it from there when I need it, except in preparation for tomorrow's dinner I brought almost two dozen logs.

I couldn't believe Frances gave me at least ten times more firewood that I was expecting. Now I have firewood that will last me to Memorial Day if I start burning it every weekend from now on. My chimney will look like one of the stacks of the refineries in the area, smoking.

Miriam asked if she could bring refreshments. I told her of course, she may have a better idea of what my neighbors will enjoy than me; she has known them longer than I have. I am looking forward to what she is going to bring. She told me not to buy wine because she is going to take care of quenching our thirsts, and more. The "more" scares me a little. Now that I have spent more time with her, it would not surprise me if by the end of the night, we will be drinking fireballs. She is the liveliest habitant of our little street, and she knows how to get a party started. Last summer when she invited me to her annual BBQ, she said that she was inviting a few friends for a barbecue. She told me to be at her house at 5:00 p.m. on the last Sunday in July and make my way to the backyard. I guess when people are retired it doesn't matter which day of the week they have a party. The rest of us mortals just need to show up to work barely awake. When I stepped outside the house to go to her place, there was a super duty dual cab pickup truck with a trailer parked in front of her house. Both had flashy signage. On the trailer you could read "Tommy's The Best BBQ on Wheels, Bringing the Flavor to Your Table", next to a picture of Tommy holding a serious BBQ fork with a big piece of beef on it. I could hear country music playing getting louder as I crossed the street. When I made it to the backyard, the place was full. Just like Rob, I thought most of her guests and friends were going to be around her age, but to my surprise there were people in their early 20s to their 80s. I guess Rob was there, but I do not remember seeing him. How could I have missed him? He can stand out in a crowd being at least six feet two inches tall, with an athletic build and dark brown hair cut short. I introduced myself to two or three of the guests and after that I settled into the table where the rest of the Sea Foam Lane ladies were having mint juleps. Maybe that was my mistake. I should have mingled a little more and met a few more people. Lesson learned: circulate around a party before settling in with the people you know. Tommy was grilling ribs, chicken breasts, brisket and sausages. He looked older than his picture on the trailer and many pounds heavier. There was a table with side dishes and condiments. There were two bartenders taking care of the bar, one serving mint juleps from a pitcher and the other preparing drinks. Besides cocktails there was wine and beer. Miriam was wearing a cowboy inspired outfit: stylish denim jeans, brown boots, a checkered short sleeve blouse and a cowboy hat. I left the party at eight since I needed to take care of a few things before going to bed. Later Miriam told me to my surprise that five of her hardcore friends did not leave until the next day. They played dominos until 3 a.m. and then just stayed for breakfast. I remember the next day when leaving for work seeing two of them coming out of her house walking like zombies and getting into the taxi that was waiting. I hope when I retire, I have the same stamina they do.

IT IS time to start cooking!!! I fetch my favorite apron, a gift from my mom for my 33rd birthday. It was her last present to me and what it makes more special is that she sewed it. The fabric pattern has little red flowers, which are perfect for disguising any spots from my cooking. I have the tendency to splash stuff all over when I cook. My counter space is limited, it is a small house with a small kitchen, but the owners had the foresight to build a small island with cream-colored ti-tles with yellow and cobalt blue designs. The island provides valuable extra space and somehow it reminds me of Tuscany. I never have been in Tuscany, maybe I'm reminded by the pictures from the interior design magazines that my dentist keeps in his office. One day I must go to Tuscany and find out what a traditional Tuscan kitchen looks like.

I like to get out all the pots, bowls and pans that I will be needing before I start cooking. Otherwise, I find myself walking around the kitchen with ingredients on my hands looking for pot. My sisters always give me a hard time for it, and last time we cooked a meal to-gether they said cooking is not project management. I need a decent size pot to boil the chicken breasts, a pot to soften the dry chiles, and a big frying pan to cook the pork.

I BOUGHT PORK SHOULDER, a piece of pork loin and a slab of ribs. I remember *abuelita* (grandmother) Amelia cutting the meat for the tamales into perfect pieces, not too big and not too small, it looked so effortless when she did it. Either my knife is not sharp enough or I haven't mastered the cutting technique. Most likely it is the former, I don't recall the last time I sharpened the knives. I have been living in this house for almost eighteen months and I'm sure I haven't used the whetstone yet. I cut the slab of ribs into individual ribs, then I cut the pork shoulder and the pork loin into small pieces. Now I remember why I don't care for pork shoulder—I spend too much time trimming the fat. Next time I will only buy pork loin because it is so easy to cut, and you do not need to be trimming it for what feels like an eternity. Maybe I should have asked grandma the name of the cut she so effortlessly cut into little size morsels. I am sure it was pork loin.

My big frying pan is heating up. I like to hear the sizzle when the meat touches the pan. The meat needs to be seared before adding salt and pepper and covering it. After a few minutes, I will check if there are enough drippings from the meat or if I need to add water for more vapor to help cook the meat without losing its moisture.

I wash the dry chiles and then remove the seeds. Grandma always roasted the chiles on a *comal* (griddle, a flat steel pan) and she did not remove the seeds because the whole family enjoyed spicy food. But I do not know my guest's preferences regarding spicy food, which is why I am removing the seeds to keep the red sauce mild. I am not toasting the chiles like abuelita did. Instead, I am putting the chiles in hot water until they are soft, a method I learned from my mother. Toasting the chiles requires paying constant attention to them, turning them to make sure they get roasted evenly and removing them from the comal just at the right moment.

The pot of water is almost starting to boil just as I finish deveining the chiles. I drop them into the pot, turn off the fire, push the chiles under the water, then cover the pot. In ten minutes they should be soft and ready to be blended.

Roland is getting a little restless. Our early outing altered his schedule. He was taking a nap and now he is staring at me as I cook away. He had enough of cooking and walks toward the back door. I will let him out to the backyard where he can entertain himself or look at the birds. This is better than monitoring my every move in the kitchen. "Come on boy go out and play." I toss his favorite squishy toy and he bolts to get it, I toss a half-inflated volleyball that he likes to carry around while he runs in circles in the backyard. He will be entertained for a while. As I close the door I see the pile of my dirty exercise clothes; it is tempting to just put them back in the basket, after all today is Christmas Eve, but I better wash them since I am running out of jogging attire.

Back in the kitchen, I rinse the chicken breasts. They are the ones with the skin and ribs attached. In my opinion the broth is tastier when bones and skin are included. I will degrease it later. In the biggest pot I have, I put the chicken, half of an onion, two carrots, a serrano pepper and two bay leaves. I grind fresh black pepper into the pot. I set the fire at medium. I like the chicken to simmer for a long time, but today I will be careful because it needs to get just to the point where it is cooked enough to be able to be shredded. I cannot overcook the chicken because tomorrow it needs to boil for a few more minutes with the rest of the ingredients for the green pozole.

I look into the pot where the dry chiles were submerged in the hot water. They are soft, ready to go be blended with the fresh garlic and black pepper—the ingredients for the red sauce that will be added to the pork that I have cooking in the frying pan. Because I am looking for a sauce consistency, I will need to add several cups of water. If I was preparing mole, I would add less water and more spices. Mole is denser, some recipes call for a paste consistency. I push the button on the blender and after a few spins of the blades all the ingredients become the red sauce for the tamales. I check the consistency and it looks like more water is needed. I give it few more spins. Now the sauce is ready to be poured into the frying pan with the pork, letting it simmer for a while.

It has been several minutes and the aroma of the pork in the red sauce starts to fill the kitchen and reminds me of the carnitas that my grandma prepared to celebrate my cousins Isabel and Elena's quinceañera celebration. When my twin cousins turned fifteen years old, my grandma had one of the pigs killed to prepare carnitas to feed the party attendees. That summer my sisters and I learned that nothing from the pig goes to waste in a traditional Mexican household. We were allowed to see the entire process, from the slaughter of the pig, to cleaning it and then preparing the different dishes: sausages made by filling the intestines with the cooked blood, *chicharrones* by frying the skin until it becomes crispy, red pozole with the head, and carnitas that are prepared by frying the rest of the pig on its own fat (lard) and juices. It was quite an event. We also learned that our sweet sixteen parties were modest celebrations compared to the elaborate event of a quinceañera party. Which for me was fine because I never liked too much attention.

The aromas of melding flavors when cooking my family recipes always bring back the memories of Easter vacation, summer vacation, and Christmas at my grandma's house. It was quite an ordeal to get to her house located in central Mexico, in a small quaint community nestled in the mountains covered by pines. We flew to the nearest airport after having made several connections, and then had to take a taxi to the bus station and then travel by bus making countless stops until we reached our destination. For some reason it seemed we were the last stop, but in later trips I realized that there were at least five more stops on that line before the bus could turn around and retrace its route. Sometimes we were lucky, and a family member would be waiting for us. My grandmother had an old pickup truck used to go to the fields, but it was not reliable to make it to the city. The long journey was forgotten the moment we arrived at the picturesque town. The houses were painted in red (burgundy) at the bottom, and white at the top. I remember the red tile roofs and the cobblestone streets. I recall how after the afternoon rains, the cobblestones streets became slippery and the smell of wet earth that impregnated the town. I was amazed how my grandma could tell it was going to rain just by seeing the clouds coming over the mountain, the direction of the wind and the smell of the wet dirt even if the rain was a few miles away. I do not recall a time that her forecast was wrong.

My grandmother's house was one of the oldest in town and its walls were made of adobe, almost two feet thick. Her kitchen looked so different from ours. On our first trips to visit her, the kitchen still had a *fogón* (a set cooking fireplace) in one corner. There was a small window in the wall towards the ceiling to let the smoke out and the section of the walls next to the fogón were black. Early in the morning the tortillas were made on a comal sitting on the fogón and after the tortillas were done a pot with beans or with corn for next day tortillas was placed on the remnants of the fire to start cooking them.

Some of the artifacts in my Grandma Amelia's house were foreign to my sisters and I. The *metate* and *molcajete* were on top of the list. The first is used mostly to grind corn and the second to prepare salsas.

Of my favorites artifacts was a set of *cazuelas* (red clay pots) nestled in one of the corners of the kitchen and the rustic handmade wooden spoons in different sizes that my grandma kept in a red clay vase. The items showed signs of their use throughout the years. The *cazuelas* were blackened from the years they had been used to cook on the open flame of the *fogón*. One of the wooden spoons had a reddish hue because it had been left in a pot of mole for a while, and another's handle has been blackened because it started to burn when left close to the flame.

Through the years the kitchen was remodeled but even when it got modernized, it still was more colorful and exotic than our kitchen in Wisconsin. Ours did not have the vibrant colors of the *azulejos* (tiles) in the counters, the comales, cazuelas, metate, molcajete and tortilla baskets that you could find in abuelita Amelia's kitchen.

Those vacations in Mexico in grandma's house are some of the most precious childhood memories I have. Seeing my mother with my aunts having lively conversations, being introduced to new flavors, running to the plaza to get a popsicle, and playing with my cousins all over grandma's house for hours, or going to the bakery to get freshly baked sweet rolls are cherished memories.

It is amazing how the aromas of food bring back memories. It is like I am transported to grandma's kitchen. When tamales were being prepared for a party, there was always quite a commotion at grandma's kitchen that started the day before with the washing and boiling of the corn. The next day in the morning the corn was taken to the *molino* (mill) to have it ground into masa. The preparation always started after breakfast. My mom, aunts and grandma worked in this almost synchronized process of preparing the different fillings for the tamales.

My cousins and I played in the courtyard. Grandma's house had a courtyard and on the border was a wide hallway with this beautiful yellow and turquoise tile that you only saw in the older homes. We usually gravitated to the *corral* for serious playing. The corral was the backyard, which was enormous. For us kids it looked like a jungle, with citrus trees, avocado trees, coconut palm trees, peach trees, and all kinds of herbs and flowers. There were also chickens and pigs, which were corralled. In her backyard, I learned that the cilantro actually flowers and looks a little different when the plant reaches maturity than the cilantro we get in the store. When we walked through the door to take us to the corral, we imagined we were entering a different dimension, a different country, continent, world. That old wood door was our portal to infinite adventures. Our imaginations were limitless. In the warm days of summer, we dreamed we were exploring the Amazon jungle. We also had days that we kept it simple and played hide and seek. Usually around one or two o'clock, somebody would come and get us for lunch. As kids having a blast, we forgot that time existed. I recall my mom would scream *chiquillos vengan a comer* (children come to eat). We ran to the kitchen, and we were sent by one of my aunts or my mom to go and wash our hands all the way up to the elbows. We needed to make sure that all of us had our hands clean, otherwise we were sent back to wash them again. All of us had to go, not only the one that did a poor job. It only happened to us twice. We learned to wash our hands properly so that we could start eating as soon as possible. How funny it is that we were not hungry while playing, but as soon as we were told lunch was ready, we became ravenous.

The table in my grandma's dining room could sit eight adults comfortably or ten kids. I have two sisters, my oldest aunt had three boys and one girl, and my youngest aunt had one boy and two girls. Yes, the holidays we spent with my grandma were awesome. I think grandma used to get tired of the ten rambunctious kids by the seventh or eighth day. She would say "Lucia, Emilia, and Patricia come and take care of your kids." That was the sign that she had enough of us screaming and running all over the house. A few hours later, my aunts would go to their homes for the rest of the day and the next day come back after lunch, as they lived in the same town. I enjoyed it when my sisters and I had time with grandma without the cousins because she would tell us stories, or she asked us to help with chores like getting herbs from her garden. She explained the different uses of the herbs—which ones were for cooking and which could be used for home remedies.

Walking into the dining room that was connected to the kitchen by a small door was an immersion into the aromas and flavors of a Mexican kitchen. By one o'clock, the fillings for the tamales were ready. Each one of us used to get a plate with portions of pork in red sauce, beef picadillo and chicken in green sauce. Several baskets of fresh prepared tortillas were placed strategically on the table and we just started making tacos with what we were given on our plates. Sometimes we were given Spanish rice and beans to accompany the tacos. Those were the days when we could eat all the carbs we wanted and it did not matter. Vegetables were always served with our meals, but I do not remember too much about the vegetables, mostly they were steamed or raw sliced carrots, cucumbers, and broccoli florets. We did not resist eating them because we knew that grandma was not going to allow uneaten vegetables on our plates. No vegetables, no ice cream from the ice cream man that went by the house between four and five in the afternoon on his way to the plaza. He prepared the best key lime ice cream that I have had in my life. It had just the right amount of sweetness and lime zest. When we finished lunch, we were ready to go to the living room to watch a few cartoons while we digested our food. The rest of the day was spent going to the plaza, playing table games, or one last trip to the corral to let our imaginations run free.

Grandma, my mom, and my aunts ate lunch after us. It was always great to hear them talk about their lives before they got married and had us. There were conversations about their days in school, their old friends and relatives. They updated each other of who had another child, who moved to a different town, who had died, who had lost the husband to the lover. All the pent-up gossip was shared in those moments that they spent together in the dining room. There were exclamations of "I can't believe she did that", "Wow how things have changed!", "Oh no, he was too young to die." They would finish lunch and clear the table and wash all the dishes. It was a wonderful assembly line: one would wash them, the other rinse them and the last one dried them. Grandma would put them away and in no time the dining room and kitchen were ready for the next phase in the tamale preparation.

On the dining room table they placed the plastic bowl containing the masa, the cazuelas with the fillings, and the corn husks. At the end of the table were the *vaporeras* (large steamers). It always looked like a beautifully orchestrated process how they prepared tamales—taking the husk delicately, spreading the masa effortlessly on the husk, putting the filling on it, wrapping them just perfectly, and then placing them in the steamer. Sometimes we helped, but we were not required to help until we became teenagers. My grandma requested that boys and girls helped, we only had to take turns. She did not want ten teenagers starting to play with the masa and making tamales in interesting shapes, eating the fillings and goofing off. I enjoyed those days visiting Grandma Amelia.

OH GOSH!!! While reminiscing I forgot to put the corn husks in water. It is time for a shortcut! I am warming up some water on the stove while I rinse the corn husks. While they seem clean and ready to use, I prefer to run them under the water and separate them to make sure they are clean. After rinsing them, it is time to put them in the warm water to get them soft. I think I am back on track; the chicken is almost ready. I am turning off the fire and removing the cover to let it cool down so as to take the chicken breasts out and pass the broth through a strainer. The pork smells like I recall when grandma and mom used to prepare it. I am happy that at least the aroma is what I was expecting. It always amazes me how many flavors can be created with the same chiles just by changing their proportions or adding an extra spice. In twenty minutes, the meat will be ready and then it will be time for me to go and nap for fifteen minutes. I am not going to undertake the preparation of tamales without having a nap.

I LOVE TAKING NAPS. If I cannot take a long nap, I take a fifteen-minute nap or a Da Vinci nap. It is said that

Leonardo Da Vinci just slept fifteen minutes every few hours. I take a fifteen-minute nap and then I sleep seven hours. I do not think mankind requires me to not sleep in order to make any magnificent discovery or create a masterpiece.

Nolan is in the middle of the bed sleeping or faking that he is asleep, I think he just opened his eyes a bit. I move him to the side of the bed and he does not like it, which is too bad because this is my bed and he has his own little cozy puffy bed by the sliding door, but he prefers to invade mine. I set the alarm, and I hope soon I will be in the arms of Morpheus the Greek god of sleep and dreams. Yes, these days I only can imagine I am in the arms of a Greek god. One of my goals next year is to find myself in the arms of a mortal. A mortal from any of the cities in Los Angeles County will do. If he is willing to cuddle me until I fall asleep, I will consider mortals from Ventura and Orange counties. Of course, if he has special skills to help me get to sleep quicker while bringing a smile to my face before falling asleep, who cares if I need to go far away to an exotic land!

WHAT IS THAT NOISE? Oh, it is my alarm, my fifteen minutes are up. As I move to get up, I realize Nolan has come close to me and he is annoyed that I am moving. Kitties are so vocal when they want to be.

"Sorry Nolan, but mommy needs to go to the kitchen and keep working until those tamales are ready for tomorrow's dinner."

I feel refreshed, I am ready to take on what seems to be a monumental task. This is not the first time I have prepared tamales by myself. It is fun to prepare them with your family and friends, but I did not want to put my friends to work. This meal is one of my gifts to them. I am not going to prepare too many. I plan to make three dozen. Once I made over one hundred by myself; I think I started late in the afternoon and by the time the last of the tamales were cooked and the kitchen was clean, it was 2 a.m. But on that occasion, I made chicken, beef and pork tamales. Today I am only preparing pork. This year I bought the masa instead of preparing it from corn flour. Preparing it from corn flour is a good workout for the arms.

Ok, let's get the assembly line ready. Drained husks are in a colander clean and ready, masa is out of the refrigerator and the frying pan with the pork in red sauce is ready. I was so happy to find this place in town that makes fresh tortillas every day, and during the holidays they sell masa for tamales. Their claim to fame is that the masa for the tamales is made from freshly ground boiled corn. They also will sell it, if you need some when it is not the holiday season. You just need to call and place the order a few days prior to the day you need it. I wrap the tamales and put them on a platter. When I finish wrapping the last one, I stack them in the steamer.

I am trying to find my big wooden spoon or a big wooden spatula. They are my favorite tools to spread the masa on the corn husks. Where are they? I remember unpacking them over a year ago. Ok, let's look in the drawer where I keep miscellaneous kitchen items. Voila! I found them. I knew I had put them in a special place.

The first tamales are the most challenging. If I start overthinking it, I will never finish. I used to wonder if I had put too much masa or filling. Now, I just start preparing them and adjust as I go. Also, in the past I did not like that my tamales were not like the ones prepared in my grandma's house. Her tamales were uniform in size and shape. Mine, on the other hand are small, medium and large. I have learned to let go of my perfectionist tendencies and care less about the size and shape to focus on the flavors. When the tamales are fully cooked, size and shape are irrelevant, the taste of the pork in the red sauce is what matters the most.

I am ready to prepare the first tamale for tomorrow's dinner. But first I need some Christmas sounds. Through the year I have been building a holiday playlist, which includes all my childhood favorites and all my favorite songs that I have discovered through the years. I am ready! I love instrumental melodies in the background when I am cooking. But when I am relaxing in front of the fireplace with a nice fire glowing, a glass of cabernet and a book in my hands, I love listening to *The Three Tenors Christmas*.

I take a nice corn husk and I use the wooden spatula to spread the masa. The masa I bought has the perfect consistency and it is easy to spread. I put a spoonful of the pork in red sauce on top. I am tempted to start eating the filling instead of putting it in the tamale. I resist the temptation and I proceed to first fold the right side of the corn husk and then the left side. Lastly, I fold the top of the husk down and I put the wrapped tamale on the platter. Ok, that was not that bad, now I just have thirty-five more to prepare...

TIME HAS GONE BY, and I have lost track of how many songs I have listened to and how many tamales I have wrapped. There is masa left in the bowl for two more tamales and then I am done! I always enjoy this part of the process. After spreading and folding for a while, it is so rewarding to see the tamales neatly stacked on the platter. I start placing them in the steamer carefully because I do not want them to become unfolded. One of my aunts likes to tie each tamale, but I just do not have the patience to do that. I made forty tamales! I feel a wonderful sense of accomplishment when the last tamale is in the steamer. Now I just wait for the water to start boiling and then I will decrease the fire and cook them from forty-five minutes to an hour. I always like to check the tamales at the forty-five-minute mark. I still remember at Grandma Amelia's, when my mom or one of my aunts would take a tamal out, open the husk carefully, let it cool down for a minute, and then give it to my grandma to taste. If she said that it was ready, all the steamers were turned-off. If she was not satisfied with it, she would give it back to my aunt to return it to the vaporera. Grandma would tell her daughters how many more minutes to cook them until the next tasting.

That was one of the moments that I clearly remember, noticing how much attention my mother and aunts paid to the words that grandma said. Her opinion was the voice of experience. I hope when I have kids they will listen to what I have to say in the same way my mother listened to her mother. Too bad my kids will not get to meet their grandmother. And while they may experience some family cooking, I do not know if they will relate to their cousins like I did to mine. The age difference between me and the youngest of my cousins was seven years, but there were ten of us and everybody had somebody to play with.

My sister Diane got married to her high school sweetheart, David, when she turned twenty-one years old, it was almost like they were waiting for her twenty first birthday for her to be able to toast. They could have had the wedding in a country where the drinking age is not twenty-one. Diane wanted to have kids as soon as possible and she did. Within a year my first niece was born; two years later she was giving birth to her first son and after two more years to her second son. David and Diane decided that three was the right number of kids for them.

Maggie on the other hand had numerous friends and boyfriends but there was nothing serious. After graduating she landed a job in New York and after three years in the Big Apple all of a sudden she was getting married to Frank, a man that she had dated only for six months and that seemed to be totally the opposite of her. The second surprise came when she became pregnant and stopped working to spend time with the baby. Then the second baby arrived. As for myself, I am here alone, and by the time I have kids my nieces and nephews will all be teenagers, and they may just see my kids as crawling bunches of diapers.

I SET the timer for forty-five minutes. While the tamales are cooking, I will wash the dishes and straighten the kitchen. My sister Maggie says that when I cook the kitchen ends up looking like the scene of a science experiment gone wrong. Everybody has their cooking style and mine is messy, but the result of my mess is a delicious dish. I am looking forward to getting off my feet. I am tired, and as soon I am done with the dishes, I will make a fire in the living room fireplace and relax for a while. Maybe today is the day I will finish the romantic novel that I have been reading for months. The story takes place in the early 1900s in Europe- I love stories that trigger my imagination to travel in time. I fill the left side of the sink with soapy warm water and put in the dirty bowls, the spatula, platter and the spoon to soak while I clean the counter space. To my surprise, I have not made a huge mess.

I am washing the dishes and looking at the back-yard. It is winter, and the trees look almost the same as they did during summer: green. There are a few trees sprinkled through the neighborhood that lose their leaves but these are the exception. In Southern California we do not have harsh winters like the ones I used to experience during my childhood in Wisconsin. It was always nice to go to México to visit my mom's family and get away from the cold at home for a week or two.

I still remember the first Christmas we spent at Grandma Amelia's when I was five years old and it was Christmas Eve. It was cold but it was not freezing. I kept asking my parents when it was going to start snowing. I thought Santa was not going to stop by because there was no snow for his sleigh to sled. I cried even after my parents reassured me that Santa didn't need snow. To my surprise the next day there were gifts under one of the fruit trees in the backyard.

In my grandma's massive backyard there were dozens of trees, I only have two: a Meyer Lemon tree in one corner of the backyard and a fig tree in the other corner. I use most of the lemons, but I have eaten just a few of the figs because the neighborhood squirrels love them. They are faster at picking them from the tree than I am, plus they take advantage that I am not there most of the day during the weekdays and also that Roland cannot climb trees to chase them. I am sure that by noon they are lying down under a tree branch, rubbing their tummies after having taken a few bites from a fig.

I can see a little green just over the surface of the planters that the prior owners left. The bulbs are starting to come out. Because this is just my second winter in this house, I do not know what type of bulbs are in each planter when they bloom. I will ask Bonnie and Emma to take a look, I am sure they will know immediately.

Now that the dishes are done, it is time to prepare a

cup of peppermint tea, my favorite, and I will be ready to enjoy of a wonderful fire, courtesy of Frances. She will be happy to see the smoke coming out of the chimney, knowing that I am enjoying her gift.

The living room is full of Christmas aromas: the medley of scents from the fresh Christmas wreath and garland, and the aroma of a cinnamon-scented candle burning. I believe our brain enhances aromas that make us happy. With my tea on the coffee table next to the book that I intend to finish by the end of the week, I touch a match to the crumbled newspaper under the fatwood and see how the fatwood starts to burn. The resin in the fatwood gets the fire starting in no time. It helps that the wood was well seasoned. The glow of the fire is so lovely, it lends a beautiful warm ambience to the room.

Finally! I can relax and enjoy the peacefulness of our enclave. There are no cars going by at all times of the day like on other streets I have lived on. The only sound I hear is the birds' chirping in the morning, the squirrels jumping from my roof to the trees, and Frances' water fountains. Nolan and Roland have arrived and taken their positions in the living room. They like to watch the fire and enjoy the heat emanating from the fireplace. The room temperature is getting so cozy that I feel I can take a second nap right now on the couch. I reach for my book to start reading and the timer in the kitchen goes off; it is time to check the tamales.

I carefully remove the lid from the steamer. I tilt it sideways to prevent the condensation from dripping all over the floor or the stove. With tongs I remove one of the tamales. I learned at a young age not to try to take out one with my bare hand. It was a painful learning experience. I still remember how I screamed when the scorching vapor touched my skin, but that was not the worst part. When getting my hand out of the steamer, I touched it and burned the side of my hand. Grandma flew into action. She walked me to the sink to put my hand under cold running water. While I was sobbing, holding my hand under the faucet, she was cutting thin slices of potato. She put the thin slices of the potato[1] on my hand and then wrapped it with a clean kitchen towel. She sent me to sit for a few minutes in the living room to watch TV. Grandma was asking me to watch TV? She usually wanted us away from the TV. After a while she came and removed the potato and put a slice of onion[2] on my hand and wrapped the towel around it.

"What happened to your hand?" My mom said when she saw my hand wrapped in the towel. She and my sisters had gone to the grocery, and they were back just in time to see my predicament.

"I tried to get a tamale out of the steamer." I replied, trying to avoid her gaze. My sisters were quiet standing next to her waiting to hear if I was in trouble with Mom for having done something foolish. Maggie was smiling. She enjoyed it when Diane or I got in trouble or grounded, even if she was the one always getting sent to bed without dessert or having to do extra chores due to a mischievous deed.

"Girls take this to your grandma. What do you have on your hand, onion or potato?" She sent away my sisters and I was thankful for it, there was no need to have witnesses if she was going to give me a sermon about the dangers in the kitchen. But my mother looked really calm, and I got a sense she was familiar with grandma's first aid techniques. Techniques that to me seemed a little bit odd.

"Onion." I replied holding the towel around my hand.

"I will be back." She replied and went to the kitchen.

There was a window in the living room that opened to the hallway on the courtyard. I saw mom coming from the kitchen and going into grandma's room. She came out with a tin tube. It looked like those old tubes of toothpaste. Mom came into the living room and asked me to remove the towel and show her my hand. She removed the piece of onion and then applied the ointment from the old tube over the barely noticeable burn. She took out of her dress pocket a clean handkerchief and gently wrapped it around my hand.

As she was tying a knot, she said, "Susy, what have I told you about hot dishes?"

"That I should stay away from them and not try to move them and not to touch anything that is hot." I replied. I felt a little upset with myself because I had been told more than once, and there I was with a minor burn on my hand. I should have known better than to try getting a tamale from the steamer when the vapor was visible.

"Susy is not going to forget this lesson. She is fine, she is not even going to have a blister." Grandma said as she entered the living room.

"I will not do it again." I said before I was asked.

Mom just patted my shoulder and smiled at me. Grandma smiled and took the kitchen towel that was next to me on the sofa. She reached into the pocket of her apron, took out some cookies and gave them to me with a sweet smile.

That is why I take precautions like using tongs to get the tamales out of the pot. I put a tamale on a plate and after waiting a minute I check if it is ready. They are not ready; the masa does not detach from the husk as cleanly as when they are done. For sure, in ten minutes they will be fully cooked. I cover the steamer, set the timer for ten minutes. Then I go back to my book.

As soon as sit on the couch, Nolan comes next to

me and with those piercing blue eyes gives me an inquisitive look. Then he walks back and forth on the couch. I know the look when he wants me to pet him, so I scratch the top of his head between his ears. Now he sits on my lap and there is no need to keep prancing around seeking attention. Roland, on the other hand is on his bed just looking at the fire and giving an occasional glance at me and Nolan.

The timer goes off again and I have not read my book. I was hypnotized by the glowing fire, plus Nolan, and having zero thoughts on my mind. Did I just meditate for few minutes without even realizing it? I was not daydreaming, so I guess I was! I put Nolan on the couch, and he protests.

"Mommy needs to check on dinner." I tell my little white furball.

This time the tamales are done. I turn off the burner and partially remove the lid. I will let them cool down and then put them in the refrigerator. Grandma did not put them in the refrigerator until they were cold. She said that they would go bad if they were refrigerated right away. She used to tell us that they would not go bad if they are left out for a day in a cool place. When she was a girl, her family did not have a refrigerator and the tamales tasted good for at least thirty-six hours. After that, she did not know if they would taste good. She did not know because they were all eaten by the second day.

Now I can go back to the living room and this time start reading my book after I put more pieces of wood in the fireplace. I had forgotten how nice it is just to read and not to be concerned with time constraints.

I MUST HAVE FALLEN at sleep when I changed positions and laid on the couch to read on my back. What time is it? Oh, it is almost ten o'clock. I have a pair of eyes looking at me, inquiring why they have not been fed. I get up and give Nolan and Roland their dinner. A few minutes later, I take Roland for a quick walk around the cul-de-sac. Now that my babies are taken care of, I eat one of the tamales and put the rest in the refrigerator. It is time for me to go to bed!

CHRISTMAS MORNING

*T*uesday, December 25, 2018

WHAT TIME IS IT? There is light outside already. Oh! It is eight thirty, I had planned to get up before seven o'clock to cook the pozole. I forgot to set the alarm. Nolan is curled up next to my feet. Roland walks into my room. Poor baby, he has not been out yet. I am trying to find my slippers, get my arm in the sleeve of my fluffy beige robe and I am having a hard time. Forget it. I go directly to open the door for Roland. He is following me patiently until the door is unlocked and opened, then he runs out like a rocket to take care of his business. If he needed to go out badly, he would have woken me up.

I think I better take a shower and fully wake up before I cook the pozole. I am expecting my lady friends to be here by five o'clock. I have ample of time to finish everything for Christmas dinner.

After a quick shower, I am back in the kitchen. I am hungry and microwave a tamale. My grandma would be appalled that I am not reheating the tamales using the steamer or the grill. There is no time for heating up tamales abuelita style, I need to focus on the second dish for today's dinner. Nolan comes to the kitchen and rubs himself against my legs and then he goes away, walking stylishly as cats do.

I take the chicken broth out of the refrigerator. All the fat has solidified on the top, it is so easy to remove it. I open the cans of hominy and rinse it.

Time to prepare the pozole sauce. I need cilantro, onions, garlic, serrano chiles, tomatillos and jalapeños in vinegar. After rinsing the cilantro, I peel the onion. It is not a sweet onion! My eyes start to burn. I am sure I grabbed an onion from the sweet onion pile. Maybe somebody left a regular yellow onion in the wrong pile. This onion is strong, now tears are running down my cheeks. If somebody sees me like this, they would think I received horrible news.

I am done peeling and cutting the onion in quarters. I rinse two serrano chiles and take the ends off. Since they do not smell hot, I am not going to remove the seeds. As for tomatillos, I usually like to buy the ones that are sold loose, but the store did not have them so I had to buy a bag of tomatillos that are a little smaller. One advantage is that I do not need to cut them before blending them. The flavor is the same. After I remove the husks and wash them, I put them with the rest of the ingredients in the blender.

I find mouthwatering the aroma of a recently opened can of jalapeños. The memories of bean burritos with slices of pickled jalapeño chiles never fails to come to mind. Now I am craving a bean burrito. It is good that I do not have flour tortillas nor beans, and there is no way I am going to leave the house to go to the store to get tortillas and beans. I need to focus on finishing the task at hand.

I add several cups of broth from the chicken to the

blender and push the button. Now the tomatillos, serrano chiles, onion and cilantro are liquefied. I wait to taste the sauce before adding pickled jalapeños and some of the vinegar from the can. It is always better to have a sauce that needs more chiles and not one that it is super-hot. I love this powerful blender, it takes care of any sauce in no time. Carefully I remove the lid of the blender and resist the temptation to smell its contents, another lesson I learned the hard way. Once I was preparing a habanero hot sauce, I removed the lid and I got close to the blender to take in the aromas. I took in the hot spicy air that came out of the blender and my sinuses were not happy for an hour. Now I remove the lid and grab a spoon to taste the salsa, resisting all temptation to get close to the blender and inhale the aroma. I taste the sauce and it is not hot at all. I drop in two jalapeño chiles and add a quarter cup of vinegar from the jalapeño can into the blender and push the pulse button few times. I taste the sauce and now it is mild, no more chiles needed. Next, in a pot I pour the sauce, add the shredded chicken, the hominy, and a few cups of the chicken broth. I let this simmer for thirty minutes. At the end of the half hour I will bring it to a heavy boil for two or three minutes.

My family always garnishes the pozole with radishes, onions (yes, more onions) and cabbage. While the pozole simmers, I slice the radishes, mince an onion and chop half a head of cabbage. I also cut limes and remove the seeds. While seedless lemons will do, I want to keep it as close as I can remember from the memories of having the green pozole at Grandma Amelia's.

Today it is cloudy and foggy, and the temperature dropped significantly from yesterday. After all it is winter, a mild California winter. I guess we will be seeing the sun sometime in the afternoon. I cannot imagine living in a place where there is fog every day, or it is cloudy and rainy most of the year, I enjoy foggy mornings now and then. A little variety in the weather patterns doesn't hurt.

Roland is running around and jumping in the back-yard, I think he is chasing a butterfly. Shortly he will be interacting with the squirrels. He occasionally barks at blue jays. Roland doesn't like it when they try to hide peanuts in the planters or retrieve the peanuts already hidden. The backyard is Roland's territory, and he is a zealous guardian of his domain.

FOOD, DRINKS, GOSSIP AND A REVELATION

$\mathcal{E}$verything is ready for our neighborhood Christmas dinner. Lesley stopped by on her way to one of her kids to celebrate Christmas. She dropped off the desserts and they look amazing. I do not know if I will be able to restrain myself from eating one or two cookies before dinner. The aroma of the fresh gingerbread man cookies is like nothing I can remember. I have to count slowly to ten and step away, otherwise my friends will only find crumbs. The yule log cake is a masterpiece. Only in dreams could I make something so pretty and so decadent. Satisfying my sweet tooth will have to wait for the dessert hour.

Miriam called me earlier asking me if she could stop by at four thirty to set up the bar. I said "sure." When we hung up, I thought, *the bar?* There are only five of us and she is setting up a bar, this will be interesting.

I placed the appetizers on the kitchen counter between the kitchen and the dining room. There are some crackers, cheeses, a vegetable tray and a few dips. If somebody needs to eat vegetables, they will need to eat the ones in the vegetable tray. I do not have any vegetables to accompany the tamales.

I am in ready to drop a match on the crinkled newspapers in the fireplace and start a fire when I see Miriam walking across the street. It must be four thirty. She is rolling a plastic crate with the left hand and with her right she is carrying a six pack of wine. On top of the crate is an enormous Christmas gift bag. I rush to go outside to open the gate for her.

"Dear Susy, you are learning. Are you also monitoring the comings and goings of your neighbors like Emma and Bonnie do?" She says with a big smile as I open the gate. I can hear the clinking of the bottles she has in the crate.

"Not really, I was just getting ready to start a fire when I saw you, and I didn't want you to struggle getting the gate open."

"I believe Bonnie and Emma will not be waiting until five o'clock to show up at your doorstep. After seeing me come earlier, they will be wondering if they got the wrong time, and they will not want to arrive late."

"I don't know about that. Let me help you with the wine." I look closer at the wine carrier and there are only two bottles of wine. The rest are liqueurs or mixes.

"I bet you a bottle of wine that they will be here within fifteen minutes." Miriam said with this expression of total certainty.

"Ok, Miriam, one bottle of wine. I would like a bottle of old vine zinfandel." I say without hesitation.

Miriam smiles and looks at her watch and without blinking says "My dear, it is four thirty-one, they will be here no later than four forty-six. I like red blends; I will text you a list of my favorites. Where would you like me to set all the goodies?"

"You can put them on the island. Let's make it the bar for tonight." Miriam starts unpacking the crate. She has sparkling and still bottled water plus a bag of ice. I had made ice for the last two days just in case we needed it, but I am glad she brought more. She also has a martini shaker, a strainer, a long spoon, a double-sided stainless-steel jigger, and other bar utensils. She takes out bottles of gin, tequila, vodka and rum plus a bottle with clear contents.

"Miriam, what is this?" Intrigued, I ask of the content in the label-less bottle. I wonder if Miriam is into distilling her own moonshine.

"Simple syrup, one part water and two parts sugar. This bottle is my personal recipe for margarita mix. This is my mix for fruity drinks. This one is just lemon juice and the last but not least is my piña colada mix. I also have vermouth for martinis. Do you think this is enough?" She asks after rattling off the list of all the spirits and mixers she has brought; her exuberance is that of a kid telling you what toys he got from Santa.

"Yes, Miriam, I think you have everything we may wish for tonight. I still cannot imagine we will be drinking that much." I reply. She has liquors that would last me a whole decade if I never entertained. I have some friends from work that would make this bounty disappear in no time.

"Sweetie, do you have ice?" Miriam asks me as she takes out a big copper bowl from the crate. In that moment the doorbell rings. Miriam says, "It is before four forty-six and they are here, you owe me a bottle of wine."

"Yes, I have more ice. Maybe it is Frances and not Bonnie and Emma."

"Open the door and we will see. You still do not know well those two." I go to open the door and Frances is standing there ready to come in. But my thought of not having to give a bottle of wine to

Miriam is short lived, because as I am inviting Frances to come in, Emma is almost jogging to get to my house.

"Wait!" Emma says as she opens the gate. Bonnie is behind her with an antique crystal jar containing the eggnog. Maybe it is a family heirloom because she is walking slowly like she is carrying a basket on her head while stepping over eggshells; she is intensely looking at the jar as if she could control the eggnog from spilling over with her sight.

"Hello ladies, come in!" I reply keeping the door open and holding Roland back, I cannot allow that his exuberance in greeting our guests may cause an unfortunate eggnog accident.

I close the door behind me, and Miriam is standing in the kitchen door threshold with a big grin on her face. She points to her watch and then winks and goes back into the kitchen. I look at my activity tracker. 4:43 p.m. it reads. Miriam was right. I owe her a bottle of wine. I sure hope the list she gives me includes some reasonably priced bottles. I cannot afford expensive rare wines. I don't think blends are that expensive, but I am not a wine connoisseur.

I see Frances has brought a big red bow and is placing it on the wood next to the fireplace. I guess it is her way of telling everybody that the wood was her Christmas gift to me. I get close to the fireplace to finish building the fire and I thank Frances one more time for the wood she had delivered. She smiles as she looks around the living room and says, "You have done a wonderful job at decorating the house for Christmas. The idea of hanging a wreath on the inside panel of the entry door is a great one; you get to enjoy the aroma and see it. Thank you for hosting dinner tonight."

"I am happy we are sharing today's dinner. Finally, I get to cook for you guys." I say as I light one of those long matches for fireplaces.

We go to the kitchen to join the rest. I am happy to see everybody has made themselves at home and found where the glassware is. Miriam has put ice in the big copper bowl she brought and placed the bottles of mixers in it. My guests are enjoying the appetizers.

"Ladies, thank you for coming. We will be having dinner in half an hour. I cooked tamales and chicken pozole soup using my Grandma Amelia's recipes, I hope you like them."

"Home cooked tamales are the best. You do not have to worry we will like them." Bonnie is quick to reply.

"Let's start the party, who would like a drink?" Miriam says as she holds a martini shaker in one hand and the wine opener in the other.

While I have lived here for almost a year and a half, I only have been in a few gatherings with my neighbors. I do not know if they drink regularly or if they prefer wine over mixed drinks. I guess I will find out tonight. I know Miriam likes everything! It looks like Bonnie and Emma are going to have red wine. Frances is pouring sparkling water in a glass.

"Miriam, could you prepare me a drink with your special fruity mix?" I ask. Miriam is delighted somebody is asking her for a drink.

"Miriam, I would like a martini!" Frances places her order.

"Ladies, today you are in for a treat, the best bartender of the 2014 class is at your service." She says proudly. I am not surprised that she has taken mixology classes. I knew she also took cooking classes in a prestigious culinary school in Washington. I admire Miriam's zest for life.

"Now that everybody has a drink, I would like to propose a toast to our gracious host, Susy." Emma says as she raises her glass.

"Thank you for being here. I am so happy we are together celebrating this day. Cheers!" I reply as I raise my glass.

"Cheers, cheers." The toast is followed by the sound of the glasses clinking against each other.

We have been talking about our family traditions. I glance at the clock on the microwave oven. It is already six thirty. I lost track of time and the half an hour turned into ninety minutes. Nobody seems to mind that we haven't had dinner yet. Between drinks and lively conversation we have forgotten all about dinner. It is time to heat up the pozole and the tamales. I have the pots ready on the stove, I just need to turn the fire on. In a few more minutes and we will be eating.

I do not know if it is the effect of the red wine, but Bonnie is all of a sudden animated, discussing their eggnog family recipe. I think it is the red wine that is making her carefree, her cheeks are taking on a nice rosy color.

"DINNER IS READY!" I announce to my guests as I am getting ready to pour the pozole in a serving bowl.

"Susy, do not get dirty more dishes, we can serve from the pot if you do not mind." Frances recommends.

Everybody else nods their head in agreement. I go to the dining room and get the bowls I had placed on the table. Frances is the first one to serve herself, then the sisters, Miriam, and me.

Now that we are at the table I tell my guests, "My family garnishes the pozole with radishes, onion and cabbage, and some of us like to squeeze lime on it." There are two plates with fixings on the table, everybody puts a little of everything on. We are getting ready to start eating when the doorbell rings. We freeze, our spoons are so close to our mouths.

"Susy, do you have a camera to see who is ringing

the doorbell? It is strange to have unexpected visitors at this hour on Christmas." Miriam inquires.

"No, I do not. I just need to do this the old-fashioned way and open the door." I call Roland to be next to me as I open the door. Roland comes close to me, and his tail is wagging. I guess he does not sense any danger. I say, "just a second," and I open the door slowly, with my body leaning against it.

"Susy, it is me, Lesley, could I come in? It is cold out here." Lesley says as I open the door no more than an inch.

"Oh, sure Lesley. Please come in. What happened? I thought you were going to be at your son's place." I am a little embarrassed for keeping her out while I was preparing for the worst. Roland wiggles his tail and goes to the living room to his bed. Nolan makes his appearance, seeking some attention from the arriving guest and then proceeds to join Roland in the living room where the fire is at its best.

"Well, I arrived at my son's house at three, we had dinner at four and we were done with all the excitement by six. I see my grandkids every day. I decided that it was time for me to come and join you guys. I did not want to miss the whole party." She says as she sits on the empty chair at the table. Everybody is happy to see Lesley.

"Lesley, would you like some pozole?" I ask. You never know, she may be hungry.

"No dear, thank you, I ate too much at my son's and I want to save the room I have for a tamale. But if you don't mind, and if it is not too much to ask, I would like a bowl of pozole to go."

"Not at all." I make a mental note to get ready a take-out container for later. And without further ado everybody starts to eat now that we all together.

"Susy, you do not have a camera monitoring your

door or your back patio?" Miriam asks, she is persistent.

"No, I do not. Should I?"

"I am of the opinion to be prepared, and not to wait for something to happen. I had my cameras installed last year when I got the alarm system. I travel several times per year, plus come and go during the day. Our street is quiet. There is no through traffic, and it is kind of hidden from the main street. This could make it a target for people trying to break in because it is secluded."

"Wait a minute! Then if you have cameras, do they record constantly or only when there is activity?" Lesley asks. I never have seen her so inquisitive.

"They are recording all the time." Miriam replies.

"Have you checked the footage for the night the yellow car was left on the street? Do you know who parked it?" Emma's tone reminds me of a police investigator.

"Yes, I saw the footage. Can I finish my pozole before I tell you what I saw? Nothing that can resolve the mystery." Miriam replies as she takes her spoon and keeps eating. We know that she is not going to reveal anything else until the bowl is empty. I can tell there is tension in the room. These ladies monitor our block through the sheer curtains of their windows. The fact there is something that they don't know has them wondering what Miriam's cameras captured the night the yellow car was left on the street. I do not know if Miriam is doing this intentionally to let them wonder and see who will be the first one to ask her to tell us once and for all what she saw. It seems like she is eating slower, taking her sweet time. Or maybe it is just the rest of us that want to finish quickly and are eating faster. She is the last one to finish eating.

"Ok, time for the details. Lesley, would you like

something to drink?" Miriam asks. I forgot to ask Lesley if she would like a refreshment when she came in. One bad point on my hostess scorecard.

"What there is to drink?" Lesley inquires, she had not seen Miriam's traveling bar in the kitchen.

"There is a full bar in the kitchen, and we have the best bartender we could ask for." Bonnie chimes in.

"Ladies, how about if we go to the kitchen, refresh our drinks and get some tamales." I recommend. Everybody gets up and proceeds to the kitchen with bowls and spoons in hand.

"Please just leave everything in the sink, thank you." I instruct them.

"Dear friends, I was thinking for our next course and the discussion of the footage; we should have some margaritas! What do you think?" Miriam asks and gets the ok from everybody. She turns to me and asks, "Susy, do you have a pitcher? There is no point at preparing them one at a time."

"Yes, I have a pitcher." I open one of the cabinets and there is a big plastic pitcher, it is yellow with this awful pattern. I got it in a white elephant gift exchange at work. We are going to be in trouble if Miriam makes the whole pitcher, there will be at least to two margaritas per person. Not as if she prepares the whole pitcher, we need to drink them, but if the margaritas as good as my first drink then we are in trouble.

"Now we are talking, tamales and margaritas, what else could we want for Christmas?" Lesley says.

"I want to know what Miriam knows about the mystery car." Emma is having a difficult time waiting for Miriam to reveal her findings.

"Ok, I will tell you. I checked the recording, and the car was dropped off at 3:15 a.m. Bonnie you were right about the time. Also, the driver is a tall man. You cannot see his face because he was wearing a sweatshirt with a hood. Plus, the lighting of the street is not that good. He got out of the car, then looked inside like he was searching for something. He took a gym bag from the passenger seat. He closed the door. Then opened the trunk and either took items from, or put items in the gym bag. I could not see because he had more stuff in the trunk. He put what looked like a trash bag on top of something blocking the view of what he was doing. He closed the trunk, took out his phone, and looking at it made a call. He locked the car and then walked away and turned left on the street. Where are the glasses for the margaritas? Who wants salt on the rim?" And just like that she finishes describing in great detail what she had seen and then changes the topic.

Based on the inquisitive looks of my guests, I believe that before anyone tells Miriam whether they want salt on their Margaritas, they will want to know more. Her captive audience is not satisfied with her story and there are questions needing answers.

"Miriam, I do not understand. The car is parked in front of my house, and you can see from your house what is going on outside my house, how is that?" I am intrigued. Is she the biggest snooper of the block? She is always commenting about Bonnie and Emma. They do not have high-tech devices to monitor our little street. There is total silence in the house. Only the fire crackling in the living room can be heard. Everybody is waiting for Miriam to answer.

"When I bought the security system, the security company had a special, a state-of-the art camera system. The offer included ten small exterior cameras. I did not need more than two or three cameras in the backyard, and one on each side of the house. For the rest, I told the installer to position them in a way that the whole cul-de-sac could be monitored." Miriam finishes talking and claps her hands behind her back, almost like a little girl trying to look innocent.

"Are you invading our privacy?" Emma asks with a serious look on her face.

"If you are asking if every day I sit down with a bag of popcorn in hand and look at the recording to see your comings and goings, to check what time you come out of the house for your mail, or any of your other personal business, the answer is no. Are there any other questions?" Miriam looks around the kitchen waiting for somebody to ask her something else. Now she has a guilty look on her face. She reaches for the bottle of tequila and pours half of the bottle in the pitcher, then grabs the bottles of the lime juice and simple syrup and pours some of the liquids into the pitcher. She is not bothering to measure any of the ingredients. With the contents in the pitcher, the questioning continues.

"Why didn't you tell us the day we were looking at the car? Why did you not say you could check the recording?" Frances asks but her tone is neither inquisitive nor angry.

"Because I was afraid of your reaction. I should have shared it with you earlier. I should have asked you even before installing the cameras. I did not think too much of it at the time. As I said, I prefer to be prepared than to wait for something to happen. As private as our little street is in this small community, and it feels like a small town, we are part of one of the largest metropolitan areas in the country, and things happen in a city like ours. But the day the car was left on the street, I was happy I could see what occurred during the night. I wanted to share it with you but I feared what your reaction was going to be. If you feel your privacy has been invaded, I will have them reinstalled where I do not see beyond the section of my sidewalk." Miriam replies as she pours us margaritas and passes out the glasses.

Lesley interjects. "I vote for the cameras to remain installed. I like that our little street is being monitored. Ladies, we are a small group of women living alone and it is important we watch out for each other. Every time I see Frances going for a walk with Susy, it warms my heart. I enjoy the friendships we share and how we help each other in times of need. I know sometimes I get too busy with the grandkids, but Frances, I would love it if you came along when I take my grandchildren to the park or to some of their activities."

"Lesley, I would love to do that. Miriam, I do not mind the cameras, I am thankful you thought about making our little place safer." Frances replies.

"I do not mind the cameras. Just promise me, you will not be posting any footage of me coming out of the house in my bathrobe with curlers on my head to get the newspaper. I do not want to be the next viral video on social media." Bonnie says.

"I am ok with keeping the cameras the way they are." Emma adds to the discussion.

"I will not share with anybody the footage of what goes on in our daily lives. I pray that I never have to share the footage with the police. Susy, you have not cast your vote regarding the cameras." Miriam says as she looks at me.

"Well, I am ok with the cameras if you ladies promise me you are not going to run to Miriam's house every Monday morning to sit and look at the footage and analyze my social life or lack thereof. Can you promise me that?" I say this as I raise my margarita to ask for their pledge. They raise their glasses and say, "we promise."

"Miriam this is an excellent Margarita! Strong, and with just the right sweetness to it!"

"Thank you Bonnie, glad you like it! Cheers my friends!" Miriam says with a big smile on her face. The guilty look is gone.

"Ok, who is ready for some tamales?" I inquire.

"We are." My guests reply in unison.

I am taking the tamales out of the vaporera and placing them on their plates. The last one to get her tamales is Miriam. She has an impish grin on her face and in an almost whisper she says, "I believe your social life may be changing soon."

"What do you mean?" I say.

"Well Rob seems interested in you. I went to visit his mother yesterday and he happened to stop by to drop off groceries. He couldn't stop asking me questions about you." I can see in Miriam's eyes that she is analyzing my reaction. It is surprising, she met Rob and the twins three years ago and now she even hangs out with their families.

"Miriam lets go to the dining room, the others are waiting for us." I suggest. Miriam follows me to the dining room.

"Did I just hear that Susy has an admirer?" Bonnie asks with a mischievous smile while everybody else is waiting to hear more.

"Well Susy, if you want to share with the group, go ahead, or just tell them that your romantic life is none of their business." Miriam knows how to stir the pot. Her comment is intended to push me to talk about Rob. She knows our neighbors are not going to let go of this conversation until they hear more.

"Is the admirer the handsome and sophisticated man that brought you the poinsettias?" Lesley inquires. She just added a piece of information that will trigger more questions about my romantic life. I am debating if should I tell them: "Start eating because your tamales are going to get cold!", or just share my past and my potential date with Rob. Maybe it's time that they learn something more about me.

"I didn't tell them." Miriam volunteers.

"Tell us what?" The women say in unison.

"Emma, since when do you talk with your mouth full of food?" Bonnie is appalled that her sister just spoke after putting a piece of tamale in her mouth. Emma gives her one of those looks that we have seen more than once.

"Ok, ok ladies. Please start eating and I will tell you about Taylor."

"And Rob and Josh." Miriam adds.

"Wow Susy, three suitors. Please tell us." Frances puts her fork down and clasps her hands in front of her while she is resting her elbows on the table. I wonder if Bonnie will mention that a lady does not rest her elbows on the table while eating.

"I do not have three suitors." I say in hope their imaginations stop running wild.

"You have two, Rob and Josh." Miriam interjects happily.

"Who is the handsome guy that dropped off the poinsettias? Can we start with him?" Wow, Lesley is persistent.

"Yes, Lesley, I can start with him. His name is Taylor, and he is my ex. As you noticed Lesley, he is handsome and sophisticated. He is also afraid of commitments and was not interested on taking our relationship to the next level, marriage, after dating for almost five years. He was also seeing somebody else prior to ending our relationship. He stopped by the other day to bring me the gift and try to talk after one of my friends got bamboozled into giving him my address and phone number. I was going to put the plant in the trash, but Miriam stopped me."

"By the way Lily loved it. She was so happy." Offers Miriam.

"Lily Capadano? I taught three of her kids fourth grade."

"Bonnie let's not change the conversation." Emma says while Miriam just confirms with a nod that it was Lily Capadano.

"I was for a long time depressed; it was a train wreck. When I bought the house, I was just starting to get over the whole ordeal. Then the holiday season arrived, and I was not doing too well because every date brought back memories of the time we shared. I wished last year I could have been more neighborly during Thanksgiving and Christmas, but I was not feeling cheerful at all."

"Well, we are glad that Taylor is in the past and we are spending this evening together. I propose a toast for our gracious host." Lesley raises her glass, and everybody else's follows.

"I believe in 2019 Susy will find love. She is ending the year strong with two suitors." Miriam brings back the topic with a big smile on her face.

"I don't know if going out for coffee with somebody I just met will guarantee love next year. And I don't know is Josh interested in me."

"I ran into Josh at the butcher shop when I went to by some cevapcici and he asked about you. He said he likes you and would like to see you again and that he wants to call you." Reports Miriam.

"He didn't ask for my phone the other morning. Miriam, did you give him my phone number?"

"No, I did not. He asked but I told him he will need to ask you. Who knows, he may just stop by one of these days." Miriam says as she is cutting a piece of her tamale, like she knows more than what she is telling us. I wouldn't doubt she already arranged for him to "*casu-*

ally" stop by to visit her. I have the feeling that she may trying to play matchmaker.

"Well, it looks like you may have some potential dates ahead. If you don't mind Susy, I am going to go and get another tamale."

"Bonnie, please help yourself as many as you want." Say I.

"I will do the same. Susy these are delicious. You need to show us how to prepare them." Lesley says as she pushes her chair back and follows Bonnie to the kitchen to get seconds. I started eating the tamale that had been sitting on my plate and was getting cold while having the conversation about my ex and the two guys that I just happened to meet. It would be nice to go out with somebody, even if it is only for coffee or a hike. Adding a few friends that are local it is not a bad idea, given that most of my friends live on the Westside and it is almost impossible to get them to come to San Pedro during the weekends. They just give me that look when I invite them. I know what they are thinking— driving thirty-five to forty miles one way to get to my house is not on their list of favorite activities to do during the weekend after driving in Los Angeles' maddening traffic during the week. I can't blame them.

THE REST of the dinner has gone well, everybody got seconds and have been refilling their glasses with Miriam's delicious margaritas.

"Susy, promise us that next year you will host a tamale preparation party. Miriam can mix the margaritas as we cook." Bonnie asks me.

"Yes, that is a wonderful idea. I would love to learn some authentic Mexican dishes. If you don't mind sharing some of your family recipes."

"Dear friends, I will be more than happy to share

with you my family recipes. I am sure my mother and grandmother would be delighted that you learn how to prepare some of my family's favorite dishes. Let's go to the living room and enjoy the fire. Frances, thank you for the firewood. I am enjoying it immensely. Plus, ladies I have some gifts for you." I tell them.

As we get up and start making our way to the living room. I notice Emma is walking a little sideways, the holiday cheer must be getting to her. Bonnie's face is totally red. Miriam looks just the same. How much can she drink? Lesley and Frances are a little giggly. I think I'm getting a little tipsy, I will have a glass of water, then some red wine with dessert.

Nolan and Roland react to our arrival in the living room. Roland wiggles his tail. Nolan gets up from the love seat and goes and sits next to Roland, where he plots his next move. Which lady he is going to approach first seeking attention, trying to get petted. I sit next to the Christmas tree and start distributing the presents to my guests, but they want me to open first the gifts they gave me. With all eyes on me, I open the first gift as quickly as I can. It is from Miriam. The little box has an envelope inside with a gift card for the spa in the resort in Rancho Palos Verdes. Next is the gift from Bonnie and Emma. It is a square box. I open it and there is tissue paper covering its contents. Inside is a terracotta pot, but that is not the main gift. Inside the terracotta pot is a gift certificate for the best Italian restaurant in town. That was a creative way of wrapping it. Last but not least is the gift from Lesley: a red envelope and inside, a gas gift card.

"Thank you ladies for these thoughtful gifts. Now it is your turn." I start handing over their gifts. They remove the ribbons and rip at the festive wrapping paper. My present to Frances is a stylish sports top with long sleeves in her favorite color, turquoise blue. It has reflective strips. Emma gets a card to go to the movies; she loves to see movies at the movie theater. I gave a gift certificate to the local nursery to Bonnie, a true garden enthusiast. My gift to Miriam it is a certificate to her favorite car wash; her car is always the cleanest on the block. I got Lesley a gift certificate to a local seafood restaurant overlooking the ocean, she loves fresh seafood and sunsets.

Time has flown by and it was almost nine o'clock. It is a good time to have dessert. Miriam opens a bottle of red wine which it pairs perfectly with the yule log cake that Lesley baked. As a professional baker, it cannot be more perfect. The cookies are disappearing fast. Being so delicious, I cannot resist having more than one.

My friends start sharing stories about the neighborhood. Up to today day I had not been told too much about the couple that lived here before. Tonight, I am told more details about the wonderful lady who was the previous owner. Her name was Joann. They reveal the concerns they had when the house was for sale. They were close to Joann, and they were afraid of who the buyer would be, and if the new owner was going to somehow disrupt the harmony of Sea Foam Lane. They confess having had a long conversation with the realtor, one of the most trusted real estate agents in town. They told him they wanted to make sure he mentioned that the inhabitants of Sea Foam Lane were a tight group and did not like drama. I only can imagine how that conversation went.

BETWEEN LAUGHS, toasts, the crackling of the fire, and Nolan's meows, midnight has arrived.

"Ladies, I don't know about you, but I am ready to go to bed. Susy thank you for such a wonderful evening." Lesley says as she gets up and starts to walk towards the door.

"Come on Bonnie, it is way past our bedtime." Emma signals her sister that it is time to go.

"We should do this more often, get together and have a meal or tea or coffee." Miriam says as she hoists herself from the sofa. "Susy do you mind if tomorrow I pick-up my stuff, it is too late to be dragging my mobile bar home."

"Sure. Tomorrow is fine."

"Hey maybe when the weather gets warmer, we go to the park and have a picnic." Frances says as she is walking by me towards the door.

"Yes, ladies let's plan something for January."

Tonight was fun and I would like to spend more time with them. While through the months I have been able to interact with the ladies individually, it's nice to get together as a group.

Everybody is by the entryway and between hugs and goodnights my neighbors walk out into the cold air of the first minutes of the day after Christmas. I keep the door open until I see them get to their homes. Before closing the door, I take a quick look at the yellow car which is covered with drops of mist, something that you see most winter nights when you live close to the ocean. I wonder if the car still will be here by the New Year. I close the door as Roland stands next to me and the Nolan the furball is leaving the living room and hurrying up to get away from the cold air that just entered the house.

I do not have energy left to clean the place. And the last glass of wine may have been a little more than my limit. I am beyond tipsy. I take a look at the dishes in the kitchen and definitely I am not doing anything else, it is time to go to bed. I will only take care of my night routine, then get in my comfy pajamas and retire. I need a good night's rest after hosting the ladies of Sea Foam Lane for Christmas.

I am trying to sleep but I can't. Memories from Christmas with my family are showing up in my mind. I miss my mom and tears start to build up. Why is it always in moments like this that we miss the ones we love the most... I think I am falling asleep.

THE DAY AFTER CHRISTMAS

*W*ednesday, December 26, 2018

OH MY GOSH! I have the most horrible headache! It feels like my brain is throbbing. I do not want to even open my eyes, but I have to and what is the first thing I get to see? Nolan's blue piercing eyes are looking at me. The furball is next to my pillow. It is only 7:00 a.m. and I am awake. "Crazy kitty, why are you monitoring me so close?"

The day I should be sleeping late, I wake up at seven, really?

I get up to open the back door for Roland before he asks me to. I go to the kitchen and Miriam's bar is still on the little kitchen island, just as we left it last night. What am I saying? What I was expecting, Santa's Helpers to come in the early hours of the morning and clean the kitchen? It looks like all the piña colada mix is gone and there are several empty bottles of wine. The margarita pitcher is dry. How many drinks did we have? Too many based on my headache. I drink a glass of water and then I go back to bed.

It is nine o'clock and my phone starts ringing. Miriam is calling. She wants to know if she can come to get her stuff. I am not feeling that red hot. I cannot go back to sleep, and staying in bed is not helping with my misery. I am in pain. I tell Miriam to come in ten minutes.

The ten minutes go by way too fast for my liking. Miriam is ringing the doorbell and the chime is piercing my head, I am a little dramatic this morning. I manage to open the door with a smile on my face. I do not want it to be too obvious that I have the worst hangover of my 30s. "Hello Miriam!" I tell her cheerfully as I let her in, covering my eyes from the morning light. Where is the fog when you need it? I feel like one of those vampires from movies: when the first sun ray of the new day starts to melt them, or their skin starts to smoke before they burst into flames. But in my case the only thing coming out of my pores is the alcohol I had last night. I believe I smell like a distillery or the local bar just after all the patrons have gone home.

"Susy, you look like you are in bad shape." Miriam tells me. No kidding, I do not just look in bad shape, I am feeling bad.

"Yes, I am." Are the only words I can utter.

"I will be back, please go to bed or lie on the couch. Do not close the door, I will be here in three minutes, I promise." She runs out. I wonder what she is up to. Before I can ask her, she is gone. While she is full of energy this morning, I feel like I am moving in slow motion. I am starting to feel queasy. I make my way to the couch. In the living room there are plates and glasses from the night before. I feel like I am going to start spinning like a ceiling fan, which is not fun.

Miriam comes back and looks at me, "Susy are you feeling dizzy?"

"Yes, I think I am going to start spinning out of control." I reply while I cover my face with a cushion. Nolan is perched on the reading chair, monitoring my misery.

"Susy, please put your left leg down, it needs to touch the floor, it will help you stop the spins. Let me get you a glass of water. You need to take vitamins and electrolytes." I put my leg down, questioning my sanity for taking her advice but what else do I have to lose? But what sanity? My sanity was gone last night when I had the second Margarita. I don't recall if I had one or two glasses of wine after that.

Miriam sounds really calm and caring. I can listen to her steps, she always walks like she is in a hurry, short quiet, always at a steady pace.

"Please sit up Susy and drink this." Miriam gently orders. I open my eyes just to see Miriam standing there with a glass of fizzy drink in one hand and few tablets in the other. She is looking at me the same way my mother did when I overindulged eating a chocolate cake after everybody went to bed. I thought it was a good idea to raid the refrigerator at midnight and eat almost all the cake leftover from dinner—which was almost half of it. A few hours later after I sneaked back to my room I was not feeling that well when the sugar rush was gone, and I was left only with a horrible stomachache. I still remember my sister Maggie's little grin of satisfaction when my mother told me that for two weeks I was not going to have dessert or any other sweets.

"Why am I going to drink this? I got drunk with all the drinks you mixed; this may be one more of your famous drinks." I think I just sounded more like a five-year-old than a thirty-five-year-old woman.

"Susy don't be childish, this is not an alcoholic drink, it has vitamins. You need to replenish the minerals you have lost. You are dehydrated. You did not drink enough water. Plus, the sugar from all the desserts did not help either. Yes, I prepared the drinks, but you were the one that decided to drink everything, even the eggnog." I think my mom would have shown more mercy regarding my state than Miriam. But she is right I drank every drop of the cocktails and wine, even eggnog!!! I comply with Miriam's request; I drink the glass of fizzy water and take the tablets.

"Susy please rest for a little." Miriam throws over me the blanket I keep on the sofa and then she goes to the kitchen.

I OPEN my eyes and Miriam is sitting on the loveseat reading the novel that I have been trying to finish this break. I guess I fell asleep, I do not have a clue if I slept for a few minutes or several hours. There is a fire burning and all the dirty plates and glasses are gone; the place is spotless. Nolan is nestled between my legs and the back of the sofa.

"Hi, how long I have been sleeping?" I ask Miriam as I put a second cushion under my head.

"Almost three hours. How are you feeling? You must be hungry." Miriam says. She has this grandmotherly expression that is the first time I have seen on her.

"I am feeling way better, thank you. Yes, I am hungry, I think I better eat some of the leftovers." Slowly, I sit up, I get on my feet and make my way to the refrigerator. Definitely I am feeling better. Miriam is following me with a cup of tea in her hand. The kitchen is spotless. Miriam's bottles and barware are gone; all the dishes have been washed and put away. Nolan comes to the kitchen with us, he rubs himself on my legs and then goes away. Roland is lying in the sun in the back yard. I take the pozole from the refrigerator, fill a bowl and heat it up in the microwave.

"Miriam, thank you for taking care of me and cleaning the house." I say as I start the coffee maker. Today tea is not going to be enough, I need a cup of strong coffee.

"Last night was wonderful, everybody had a great time. I delivered a container with pozole to Lesley, I returned Bonnie and Emma's crystal jar, and I took away all my goodies." Miriam shares what she has done since I collapsed on the sofa.

"Wow, thank you. Did you tell them that their host was a mess this morning?"

"Oh Susy, you should have seen them, our friends were not too inquisitive this morning." Miriam is smiling as she explains.

"How do you do it? How do you drink and not get a horrible hangover?"

"Well Susy let me tell you..." She stops and I am waiting for her secret.

"Please tell me. Next time I want to do what you do and avoid feeling that my head is going to explode."

"Susy, Susy, I am going to confess. I did not drink as much as you guys did. I was your bartender; I couldn't drink with abandon like the rest of the ladies of Sea Foam Lane. People can have all these recipes to cure a hangover or protocols to avoid one, but at the end of the day you still have a hangover, and you need to suffer through it. Trust me I have tried so many things to avoid it or cure it and I have not found anything that makes disappear by magic the horrible feeling of having drunk that extra glass of wine or the eye-catching cocktail."

"I was hoping you knew something I did not. I have never seen you like you had a hangover."

"You have two choices: either you hide from the world when you have one or you put make-up on, wear the biggest sunglasses you have, and make it through the day. And on that note, I think I better get going. You are up and look way better than when I arrived; my services are not needed anymore." Miriam gives me a hug and walks herself to the door. But before closing the door, she asks me if she can borrow the book I am reading when I am finished with it. I shake my head and say, "Yes, of course."

I am just going to eat my pozole here in the kitchen. Then go and take a shower. Today I am going to take it easy: finish reading the novel that I have been reading for months and order delivery from Loretto's- a pizza sounds good. I can't believe in college I could endure two consecutive days of partying. Well those days were almost fifteen years ago. The reality is that I am not in my 20s anymore.

FAIRY TALES FADE

Friday, December 28, 2018

YESTERDAY I SPENT the day reading, and finally just before midnight I finished my book. I did not want to start the year reading the same book; I was not too happy with the ending, but at least it was not a cliffhanger. But I would not call it a romance novel because the main characters did not end up together after all. I guess it was more real than the other fairy tales I have read where the cowboy finds the woman of his life and at the end they ride into the sunset and live happily ever after. But I really enjoyed 99% of the story and I like the author's style, therefore I will be waiting for her next book.

Waking up this morning it was great to be feeling more like myself than like a nauseous rag doll. Only on one other occasion I have gotten this sick from partying too hard, and that was five years ago at my best girlfriend's bachelorette party, and I did not even drink that much.

When I woke up I looked outside and saw what a

beautiful day it was – clear blue sky, no marine layer, no smog. I thought maybe the visibility was going to be amazing to drive around the peninsula and stop somewhere to hike. As I was leaving behind San Pedro, I decided to stop by the Pacific Riviera resort to have brunch and walk on one of the wonderful trails overlooking the ocean. But being the holidays, the place was crawling with guests and day visitors. I knew it was bad news when I saw a sign that read: "Public Parking FULL. Valet Parking $25", the thought crossed my mind to turn around and forget about having brunch, but then I remembered Miriam's words "Susy, you may want to change your routine now and then. It is amazing the change in the energy of your day when you do something different." I decided that paying for parking and going to a crowded resort was going to be different. In addition, enjoying the wonderful morning, the crisp air and the spectacular ocean views was going to be something I do not do every day. It was the perfect morning to enjoy one of the most beautiful places on the Palos Verdes Peninsula.

I waited a few minutes to hand over the keys to the valet. I never had seen the place so busy, but then again, I had only been there two times. People checking out, checking in and day visitors just like me were swirling around the lobby. There was live music. A young woman in a festive red dress was playing the piano near the fireplace in a waiting area by the lobby. The music was soothing, the morning light filtering in through the ivory sheer curtains. Sitting on the several leather couches and reading chairs were grandparents and parents with kids and toddlers. At least four beautiful natural Christmas trees with golden ribbons and red ornaments decorated the room, and their fragrance inundated the room. I walked out of the lobby onto a terrace overlooking the Pacific Ocean where dozens of white and red poinsettias decorated the place; and complementing the décor were three-foot toy soldiers scattered around.

I searched for an empty seat, but all were taken. It was no surprise. After all if you are visiting this part of the country from somewhere where it is cold and snowing, our sunny seventy degrees day feels like a summer day. I have been told every year people who come to the Rose Bowl or Rose Parade decide to move to California after experiencing the mild winter days. While I did not come to Pasadena in early January for the annual events, I must confess that the climate was a key factor in deciding to accept one of the offers to work in a local company and moving two thousand miles away from home. I have some memories of watching the Rose Parade at home, bundled-up in my warmest clothes and looking through the window of our living room, seeing the snow accumulating on the driveway and street and watching the snowplow trying to keep up with the storm. I was inside my house without having seen the sun for days and on TV there were people marching with outfits that I could only wear on a late spring day. I could almost feel the sunshine emanating from the TV. Maybe that was just our old family TV overheating.

Now that I live in Southern California, I am able to take a nature walk in winter just like I did today. I walked through pathways with perfectly manicured rose bushes, trees and native plants.

At the entrance of one of the restaurants serving brunch there was a group of people that looked more like a mob than diners waiting for a table. When I made it to the hostess' podium, the poor hostess looked exhausted, but she still smiled and was polite. She did not frown when I told her I needed a table for one or if I could sit at the bar. She informed me that the wait time was between sixty to eighty minutes even if I wanted to sit at the bar. It did not bother me. After all, my original idea was to go hiking on one of the coastal trails. Now I had an excuse to go wandering leisurely around the grounds and the trails. She said cheerfully after giving her my info: "We will text you as soon as your table is available."

I made my way out of the anxious crowd and I got to the trailhead where the dirt path started. After a few steps I was looking at the cobalt blue ocean and some pelicans flying by in a long formation. I kept walking north until I reached a point where I could see the Point Vicente Lighthouse. I could not resist, and I took out my phone to take a picture, which I intend to send in my next year's campaign trying to convince my father and sisters to visit me. I stood there for a minute, just enjoying the moment. I had forgotten how relaxing it is to walk close to the ocean with the breeze in your face and seeing the ebb and flow of the waves. A rambunctious family walked by breaking the stillness of the moment. I decided to keep following the trail and soon I was leaving the hotel grounds and entering the Pelican Cove Park. Almost all the spots in the parking lot were taken; I never have seen it this crowded when I occasionally take the coastal route from work to home. Some people had just stopped to take selfies and others to venture down to the rocky beach. After a moment deciding to keep going or turn around, I opted to turn around and go back to the hotel. On my way back I discovered an empty bench and took in the views of Santa Catalina Island; it was a quiet and tranquil spot without too many passersby. It was so peaceful to listen only to the sound of the waves crashing against the cliff and to see the pelicans skimming over the water, flying effortlessly. Several butterflies went by, searching for nectar in the few bushes with flowers which gave some temporary color to the parched vegetation. Feeling the warmth of the sun on my face and the gentle sea breeze was relaxing. My peaceful moment came to an end because to my surprise, the restaurant texted me. It was good I had turned around instead of kept going, because I would have had to jog back to the restaurant instead of just walking briskly.

Brunch was quick. It was a fixed menu and short list of items a la carte. I made my selection from the fixed menu; it was a good deal and included a mimosa or a smoothie! I choose the mimosa. I scanned the restaurant and I discovered I was the only one eating alone. Most of the tables had families and there were only a few couples scattered through the restaurant. My table was in an awkward corner, a table for two. I do not think you could sit two people there comfortably, but it was perfect for me. There are advantages to dining alone, you get to sit where other people do not want to and restaurants always have one or two tables like that. From my chair I could see through a floor-to-ceiling window that overlooked the ocean. It was not an unobstructed view because the umbrellas and tables were part of the scenery, but my eyes were fixed on the blue of the Pacific Ocean. The food was delicious and the service exceptional. After paying the check, I walked out of the restaurant into a bigger crowd than the one I had encountered earlier when I made my reservation. I could only imagine what the wait was going to be for them, maybe two hours. I was happy that I had arrived late for breakfast and early for lunch, just at the right moment.

After this morning fun, now I am at home having a leisurely afternoon, sipping a cup of fennel tea and with Nolan curled up next to me on the sofa and Roland sleeping in his bed. I am just looking at the garland I hung up on the fence. It is looking a little dry and

I was thinking of leaving it until the first day of the year, but I think I will take it down tomorrow when I work in the front garden. The day has arrived when I am going to try to give some life to that bare spot that I do not want to see anymore. Only four full days before I go back to work on Wednesday. What was I thinking? Why not take Thursday and Friday off like most of my coworkers did? Oh well, I guess I thought I was going to get bored at home if I took two full weeks off.

NEXT YEAR I will invite my dad and sisters to come to San Pedro for Christmas. Diane told me she is considering a road trip to California now that the kids are older and David is starting to plan it. I could take off the last two weeks of the year to enjoy their company and have some time for myself. I already told them I will give them a tour of Los Angeles. Because traffic is lighter during the last two weeks of the year, they will get to enjoy more if they come for Christmas than at any other time of the year. Otherwise they will be stuck on the freeways driving at five miles per hour during rush hour, looking at the graffiti on the walls, the trash accumulated on the road, or the occasional aluminum ladder twisted up after inflicting damage to several cars.

I told Diane I could take care of my nephews while they go out and have a date or two. I will invite Maggie, but I doubt she would come. Her husband Frank loves going to the Caribbean for the holidays. Every year he takes them to exclusive resorts on islands that are smaller than Santa Catalina, islands that I never heard of, to some Caribbean tropical paradise that I could only dream of.

Maggie gave up getting a tree for the holidays. The first year of their marriage she went full bore decorating the house and buying a fresh beautiful "Douglas Fir." Frank surprised her with a "last minute" trip to Barbados. At the time Maggie thought it was a special event for their first Christmas together. After a few days in the resort, Frank confessed that he never likes to spend Christmas in New York nor any other place than the Caribbean. He does not like spending holidays with the family or friends and that he hoped she would enjoy his tradition as much as he did. I guess when you marry somebody after six months of being introduced in some random summer party, you will be finding a lot of things to learn about the person. When they returned to New York from their first Christmas together, the needles of the tree had fallen.

"Roland what is going on?" Roland has rushes from his bed to the entrance of the living room in full alert mode. I was so deep in thought that I did not hear that somebody had opened the gate and walked up to the door. Now the person is knocking on the door like they want to be heard all the way to the next block. Nobody from Sea Foam Lane knocks, they ring the doorbell. I open the door trying to smile to the uninvited visitor, and any trace of smile disappears when I am face to face with him. I can't believe he showed his face.

"Hi Susy, you look as beautiful as ever."

"Taylor, what are you doing here?" There he is on my porch, my ex-boyfriend. Tall and trim as ever, wearing navy jeans, a white shirt and a camel cashmere sweater. His hair short. He is clean shaven, with more wrinkles around his eyes than I recall. Did he run out of eye cream? Or has he been burning the candle at both ends? It is not my business if he looks tired. It looks like he has aged but he is still attractive.

"I was around the area and decided to stop by to see how are you doing and if you had gotten the present I left the other day. I see that you updated your wheels, a yellow muscle car. I never thought you would be driving something this flashy and a gas guzzling machine." He looks into my eyes, trying to find some emotion. I am trying to show none. *Around the area*, really? The Taylor I knew didn't like to leave his condo in Brentwood Heights except to go to work, visit his closest friend, or to go hiking Temescal Canyon in the Santa Monica Mountains. Today he just happens to drive thirty miles each way and twice this month? I was not born yesterday, *"Around the area"* it's more like "I am going way out of my way to show you I have changed."

"I am doing well, and I got your present." The words "thank you" cannot come out of my mouth. I just want to scream and tell him to get in his expensive hybrid car and drive back to the Westside. I feel like everything I wanted to say to him, the memories of those days after the breakup, are building inside me. I feel like a geyser, there is a torrent of words putting pressure in my torso, building up every second that he is in front of me. But I know if the words come out of my month, there will not be a way to stop them. There is a knot forming at the top of my stomach and the pressure is moving up to my chest. My throat is tensing. In any second, I am going to yell at him everything that I held back.

"Hey Roland, how are you doing buddy? How old is he now?" Taylor tries to reach to pet Roland who is standing behind me still inside the house. Is he trying to get me to invite him in? No way he is coming inside my house. He is already in unwanted territory! If he gets in, he will start giving his architectural opinion about the house, avoiding substance and talking about whatever he wants to talk about.

"Roland stay there, mommy needs to walk Taylor to the sidewalk." I close the house door behind me making sure the lock was not on. Just what I need today, to lock myself out and end up with a bill from the locksmith due to the uninvited presence of Taylor Halloway. I extend my arm gently to show him the gate and I walk off the porch and make my way to the path leading to the street. He is following me reluctantly. I hope Miriam's cameras are capturing this moment. I feel better now that he is not standing by my door.

"Susy, please give me a few minutes. Let's talk, listen to what I have to say."

"Are you going to tell me how you were dating at least one other woman during the last months of our relationship?" Taylor stops and he loses the color in his face, his complexion is turning pale. He is frozen like a marble statue. He is looking at me, I can see he is trying to find the right words. This is not turning out the way he anticipated. He did not know that I discovered his infidelity just days after we broke up. This is a shock for him. I am not enjoying this but it is helping to dissipate the pressure in my chest. I do not feel like I am going to explode any longer. If he is not going to talk, I will.

"Taylor, Mr. Zero Social Media, suddenly all over, celebrating anniversaries, going to summer events and partying hard. Posting selfies for the virtual world to see his happiness with Miss Selfie Extraordinaire. I could not believe it. You, Taylor Halloway, were so arrogant to leave a social media trail documenting for months your other relationships, months when you and I were still together."

"Susy let me explain to you. Just like any human, I am flawed, I made mistakes during our relationship, but I can tell you, I have changed. The Taylor you knew has evolved. I realized the biggest regret in my life was letting you walk away. I gave it a lot of thought about daring to come here to ask you for a chance to make things right." His smile is gone, his expression is pure bad acting, he is trying to show remorse. My "Ex" does not have any histrionic skills, otherwise he wouldn't be one of the best architects in town, he would be in movies.

"Taylor, get out and do not come back. Do not even drive through this neighborhood. We are done and I do not want to see you ever again. If there was a small hope of you and I getting back together, that moment evaporated when I discovered your infidelity." I point my finger towards the street and put my left hand on my hip giving him a harsh look.

"Susana, please listen to me. I deserve at least five minutes after all the years we shared." He puts his hands over my shoulders, he seems furious that I am not willing to even talk to him. The only times he has called me Susana was when we had disagreements.

"Please Taylor move your hands from my shoulders, and leave." Taylor does not move his hands. I am done with him, and I do not want to listen to what he has to say. Over his shoulder, I see Greg marching over from Miriam's house. Our eyes meet and suddenly I feel better.

"Hey buddy, take your hands off my girl!" Greg says as he opens the gate. Taylor lets me go and I walk back towards the porch.

"Who are you?" Taylor looks at Greg from head to toe and then looks at me.

"I am somebody who cares about Susy, and you better get going. You are not welcome here." The quiet guy that I met during the fog photograph expedition with Miriam has turned into this man with a roaring voice. Greg quickly moves between me and Taylor. I notice that Emma and Bonnie have come outside their house, Emma has her cell in her hand. Miriam is standing in the threshold of her front door.

"What are you waiting for? The gate is open!" Greg asks Taylor as he stands tall, looking taller than Taylor.

"Susy you will be sorry that you did not listen to me. We could have made things work. Now you are dating boys, I cannot believe it." Taylor only gives one step towards the street while Greg is clinching his right hand into a fist. I get closer to Greg because I do want this escalating into a fight.

"Taylor you never can be half the man that he is. Please go and leave us alone." I say this as I put my hand on Greg's back and I hold his right hand in mine. My heart is racing as fast as it can. My body is tensing, and my hands are getting clammy and shaky. Greg moves behind me. He puts his arms around my waist and whispers in my ear, "Do not worry, I got you." I lean back against his chest and interlock his hands with mine over my waist.

"I can't believe I wasted my time with you, Susana."

"And I...." I can't finish the sentence because Greg turns me around to face him and looks into my eyes.

"Susy, let it go, you are better than all the girls he will date in his life. His loss is your gain. Come, let's go inside. It is over." Greg puts his arm around my shoulders, he opens the door to my house, and he closes it behind him. Roland comes to greet him while Nolan scurries away into the kitchen.

"Hey Roland, how are you doing buddy?" Greg kneels in one knee, and he is giving Roland a hug. Numb, I slowly walk to the living room and collapse on the sofa. I see Taylor get in his car and pull away from the curb. The doorbell rings, Greg looks at me and with his hand indicates that I should remain where I am.

"Miriam, Susy is over there."

"Oh dear, that was something else. You should have seen Emma and Bonnie. They told your ex-boyfriend to never come back, or they will call the police. When he was getting close to his car, they added *"This is a de-cent neighborhood, a quiet street and we do not appreciate uninvited visitors."* I have not seen them with so much energy in a while." Miriam seems thrilled that there has been some excitement on Sea Foam Lane.

My eyes are getting full of tears, I can see the water in my eyes, I cannot hold the tears any longer and the first one goes rolling down my check, there is no way in stopping the rest.

"Oh! Dear everything is fine. Look at me." Miriam sits beside me. I turn to face her, but I barely can see her through the flood of tears, there are only blurry images.

"Calm down sweetie, everything is going to be ok. Greg, go to the kitchen and get some tea for Susy." Miriam orders.

"Miriam I never have been here. I do not know where the kitchen or the tea is."

"Ok, I need to do this myself." Miriam gets up and I can see she signals Greg to go and sit with me.

"Susy, let everything out. It is over, he will not be back." Greg says as he sits on the sofa and puts his arm around me. I hug him and I start sobbing.

"That's it, let it all out. Once and for all let it go." He is rocking me in his warm arms. The tone of voice his soothing. I keep crying until the last tear is out. I pull back from Greg and I can see I have left a wet spot on the shoulder of his blue button-down shirt.

"Oh sorry!" I put my hand on my mouth.

"No worries, it will dry quickly."

"Here Susy, drink this." Miriam hands me a cup of chamomile tea that I had forgotten I had. I am sur-prised she found it.

"Thank you, Miriam. This week it is the second time you have taken care of me." I reach for the teacup, and I take a sip. Miriam hands me a stack of paper napkins. I dry the trace of tears left on my face, and as discreetly as I can, blow my nose.

"That guy was here before and made you cry?" Greg asks with a tone of disbelief in his voice.

"No, he did not. I cried a lot last year when we broke up." Greg looks at me perplexed.

"Then, why has Miriam taken care of you twice?"

"Because we had an epic Christmas celebration. Between tamales and pozole prepared by Susy, and drinks mixed by the bartender extraordinaire, me. We had too much fun and the next day Susy needed my secret treatment to get rid of her hangover pronto. Anyway, we can talk more over happy hour. Come on Susy, go and freshen up and join us." Miriam clarifies.

"Yes, Susy join us." Greg says full of excitement.

"What happy hour? Thank you, but I don't feel like going out." I replied without waiting for their response.

"I am taking Greg to happy hour at the bar at the golf course, to show my appreciation for his help in setting up my new computer and getting rid of the old one. In addition, we are celebrating his new job."

"Susy come on, you will feel better, and it would be nice to have you with us." He puts his hand on my forearm and gives it a gentle squeeze.

"Susy, you have ten minutes to get ready. We are not leaving without you, and I don't want to miss out on the happy hour menu." Miriam says as she points at her watch.

"Ok, I will go but you are aware that I am not feeling well after the unexpected visit..." I say.

"Susy get moving." Miriam looks at her watch and sits on my reading chair, crossing her legs.

"I am moving." They are right. I need to get out of the house; no point in staying here rehashing what just happened.

WE ARE LEAVING THE RESTAURANT. What started out as a happy hour turned into a three hour meal after the bartender told Miriam that the chef had prepared rack of lamb as the special for dinner. We had a drink in the bar and shared appetizers. Then we moved to the dining room where there was live music, a guitarist playing Spanish guitar tunes, classical songs and some timeless popular melodies. Between salads, soups, entrees and dessert, the time flew by. I learned that Greg is moving to Austin, Texas to work for one of the multiple Californian high-tech companies with operations there. For a second, I thought it would have been great to spend more time with him and get to know him. He seems like a great guy. I also learned a little more about Miriam. She is the youngest of five siblings; her four older brothers are scattered around the globe. It appears all of them were highly successful in their fields and they were the first generation to attend college. She said she was thankful she had four brothers that pushed her to be strong and she sees the ladies of Sea Foam Lane as the sisters that she never had.

The moon is reflected over the ocean, the long silvery reflection sways with the rhythm of the waves. The contours of Santa Catalina Island can be seen in the distance. Soon we are leaving behind Palos Verdes, and we are back in the City of Los Angeles, arriving at our little enclave, San Pedro.

"Gregory, I forgot to drop you off."

"It is fine Miriam, I can walk home."

"It is almost two miles to your house." Miriam explains.

"Miriam it is only 1.6 miles to my house. I will be

there in less than half an hour. Plus, I need to burn tonight's dessert." Miriam nods and pulls the car into her driveway. We get out of the car and Greg gives a big hug and a kiss to Miriam. I thank Miriam for dinner and say good night. Greg starts walking with me towards my house. The yellow car still is there, every day looking less clean than the day it was left on our street. Now the birds have gotten to it.

"Nice ride." Greg says as he touches the hood and slides his hand over the yellow paint.

"It's not mine. Somebody left it here on Saturday and since then we have been creating stories about who the owner is and the contents of the boxes in the back seat. Stories that I am sure surpass the reality. Secretly, I hope that I get to see when the owner comes to get the car. But who knows, I may be back at the office by then."

"Whoever the owner is, he could not have chosen a better place to park it, a street with wonderful women." I just smile at his comment. He looks so different from the early morning when we met. He was so focused on taking pictures, just standing next to the tripod with the camera, talking occasionally with Miriam. He was dressed in worn out jeans, a heavy canvas working jacket with a hood and wearing dirty boots. For some reason he looked shorter. Today the Greg standing in front of me is wearing a sport coat, black loafers, sharp black denim jeans and a light blue poplin shirt.

"Thank you for what you did earlier. I do not know what..." Greg doesn't let me finish the sentence and gently touches my arm while he smiles. His smile is sincere.

"Hey, no worries, I am happy I was here. Ok, I better get going before your neighbors come out and kick me out." He says as he walks toward me, gives me a hug and a kiss, just like we had been friends all our lives.

"Good night, Susy."

"Good night, Greg." I open the gate and I am ready to go in when he says, "Susy, if I was not going away, I would compete with Josh and Rob for a date with you." He turns around before I can say anything, and in a few steps he is turning the corner by Frances' home. His comments put a smile on my face. As I open the front door I know exactly what I am going to do before going to bed.

"Hello! My little furball and my loyal Roland. I am home!" After greeting Nolan and Roland I go to the closet and take out the bag with my digital camera and connect it to the computer to remove all the pictures from it. Quickly I sift through the pictures, deleting the pictures with Taylor. I even delete a picture in which his sandals are in the background. There is one picture where most of the frame is this spectacular sunset, but he is in a corner. I am considering cropping it, but I decide it is better to delete it. I know one day I will go to a beautiful beach, and there will be a spectacular sunset and I will take a picture of it. I do not need to keep this one. I get to the last of the offending pictures and I delete them. I empty the waste basket, and they are gone forever. I feel peaceful and happy that I took care of this. The last vestiges of the Taylor era are gone. I am ready for whatever 2019 has planned for me. I see the camera and I decide to keep it in the living room because I am going to go to the cliffs and take pictures of the ocean before I go back to work.

IT IS ONLY 10:00 p.m. but I am tired and sleepy. I have taken care of Roland and Nolan and I am ready to get under the blankets. I can hear my phone ringing. I haven't checked my phone since I got texted that my table was ready for brunch. Then with the afternoon drama, I forgot to take it with me to happy hour. I am just going to ignore it; nobody calls me at this hour. I reach for the lamp on my nightstand and I turn it off.

There is the ring again. I was just falling asleep. I need to find the phone and turn it off for the night, as I intend to have a full night's sleep and I do not want to hear it chiming through the night like the foghorn.

The moonlight is shining through the windows, and I can see without turning the lights on. I walk to the kitchen where I think I left my phone, stepping on one of Nolan's little cloth mice that he likes to take from room to room when he gets in those rare moments of exuberant playing. The phone stops ringing, and it is not in the kitchen. It is not in the living room either. I hear the chime of a text message and it sounds like it is coming from the laundry room. Yes, it is on top of the dryer.

What? I have twenty texts and five voicemails. I listen to the last voicemail before looking at the texts. It is from dad, "Susy, please call your sister Maggie, we have been trying to reach you for hours. She needs to talk to you. Love Dad."

Then I go to the texts and the first text is from Maggie. It is a picture, a picture of a brunette lying sensually against pillows and cushions wearing only two wide red ribbons placed strategically over her naked body. The picture has a caption "My dear Santa your Xmas gift is waiting in NY, comeback soon." Oh! This is not good. Maggie must be devastated.

I go through the voicemails and texts, putting the pieces together of what happened during the day. It is almost midnight in Nevis and in Panama. I just text to my father and sisters telling them tomorrow I will talk with Maggie. I wonder if she has decided what her plans are after having found the sexy picture from Frank's lover in his phone. I text Maggie "Got your messages, tomorrow let's talk, sorry about Frank." Almost immediately, Maggie replies, "Yes tomorrow is fine, my fairy tale with Frank has evaporated in an instant."

I leave the phone on the kitchen island. I want to have a peaceful night and there is no point in trying to resolve things. Of the three Anderson girls, Maggie is the one that is not going to be giving second chances and will do whatever she needs to do without wasting time dwelling on things. I will wake up when I wake up. Breaking up with Taylor seems mild compared to Maggie's situation. Taylor and I were just dating, boyfriend and girlfriend, we were not even living together. Maggie has two children: Samantha four years old and Paul an unstoppable energetic two-year-old.

I could not imagine our parents being divorced when we were children. Our house was a happy house; the love between our parents was visible. Dad was always caring for my mom and she was his driving force. Mom always supported dad and was there to listen to him when the family business was not doing well. They were always there for each other; they were the perfect team. But also, I am not naive and sometimes it is better to go on different paths. Nobody benefits if two human beings only stay together for the wrong reasons, and in their efforts only make it more painful for themselves and the people around them.

All my life I have dreamed of finding somebody that I could share my life with; somebody that I could grow old with, just like my parents did. I thought Taylor was that man. Now I am glad that we broke up when we did, and after today's visit he showed that everything is about him. It feels good that I told him it was over and that I knew about his infidelity.

I look at the picture on my dresser, a group picture of our family when I was around ten years old. It was taken during a camping trip. In the background you see our tents and the pines. With the memories of that wonderful summer when our days were so simple because we were kids without any inclination of adult life, I turn the night lamp off, close my eyes and rest my head on the pillow, hoping to fall asleep soon.

GREEN EYES

S aturday, December 29, 2018

LAST NIGHT I was not able to sleep well. The first few hours were great until somebody decided it was a good idea to blast a firework. Roland ran into the bedroom and Nolan had his ears pointing toward the back of this head after the sound of the explosion echoed through our neighborhood. Maybe it was my imagination, but I think my eighty-year-old windows vibrated with the booming sound. My cat and dog were not thrilled; they kept looking at me like I was the one that lit the firework. Poor Nolan, his tail was puffed out for a long time.

I discovered last year that even with a ban on fireworks in the city, this town has some serious fireworks, and I am not talking about the ones the city organizes but the ones the private citizens decide to light-up to enhance their New Year's, and 4th of July celebrations. There are individuals that cannot contain themselves and they start lighting fireworks days before the last day of the year or on July 3. By 2 a.m. after the blast woke me up and stressed out my pets, I couldn't fall asleep. I decided to get up and drink tea before I attempted to close my eyes. At least it was not foggy outside. Finally, after the cup of tea and trying to soothe Nolan and Roland, I went to bed. I was able to sleep for four hours and in those hours I had the most surreal dreams. I do not recall having so many vivid dreams in one night.

I was dreaming mostly about my childhood and friends. But just before waking up I had a nightmare, a mélange of Maggie's predicament and the unexpected Taylor visit. At the end of my nightmare Maggie and I were trapped in a maze. The maze was made of tall bushes with thorns, we were running exhausted and out of breath through the maze. Every time we reached one of the exits, Frank or Taylor appeared to block it, and we needed to turn around and keep running. There were sections of the maze that were muddy, others were rocky. The path was never even. Every minute we spent in the maze the light was disappearing and not in a sunset type of way but in a way as if somebody was turning off the light switches one at a time and selectively. As we turned one corner we tripped over a pair of oversize gardening shears. Maggie and I looked at each other and without saying a word. We grabbed the shears and started cutting the bushes, tossing the clippings over our backs. We kept cutting until we had a hole big enough to crawl out of that section of the maze without getting hurt by the thorns. As soon as we crossed the opening to the next section, the hole closed itself. We did the only thing we could: keep cutting more branches, crossing to the next section until we finally reached the outer wall. The last hedge separating us from the world was the thickest and widest of all. We stepped out of the maze to a beautiful prairie with yellow and orange blossoms. In the middle of the prairie there was a rose garden and at the center of the garden was a fountain decorated with golden star fish and blue sea glass. Then all a sudden I was awake. I tossed and turned for a while trying to get back into the dream or at least fall asleep a little longer. I couldn't and decided to get up by 5:30 a.m. I figured it was a good time to try calling Maggie since it was almost nine in Nevis.

The call went quickly. I was surprised how calm she was. She decided to divorce Frank, and she shared that during her second pregnancy one of her friends told her she had seen Frank being extra friendly with a blonde in an upscale restaurant in downtown Manhattan. She disregarded the comment because there was not any indication that Frank was having an affair. Almost every day he had dinner at home and always spent the weekend with the family unless he was playing golf. Now Maggie was wondering that instead of going to the golf course he was somewhere else. He never took time off from work but that did not mean he was not leaving work earlier to have a rendezvous with somebody. The only time he took off to be with Maggie and the kids was at year end to his favorite spots in the Caribbean.

She was trying to reach me yesterday because she wanted to change her return ticket from New York to Los Angeles and stay with me. Even if my house is small, she thought we could manage. But later in the day she decided that she will be staying at dad's home until Frank moves out of the house. She does not want the children to see their father leaving the house, an unnecessary painful memory for them to have.

I also texted back Lesley, Frances, Bonnie and Emma, all of them were asking if I was doing ok after Taylor's visit. I was touched by how Bonnie and Emma were ready to call the police.

Rob left me a voicemail around the time I was trying to get Taylor out of my porch. He was asking if I would like to join him for coffee the next day. I will call him later and say "yes." I have been here eighteen months, and it's long overdue I start making friends and branch out, plus who knows maybe one day I will meet the special person in my life.

TWO MORE DAYS and the year will be over and there is a flurry of activity in the streets. From people taking down Christmas decorations, cleaning up garages and working in their gardens. On my way to the nursery and the home improvement center I saw a few colorful garage sales, one with the seller wearing a Santa jacket and hat, and the other with an inflatable lawn decoration collection. The seller had more than a dozen inflatables jammed on his lawn, one for every possible holiday, like an easter bunny wearing a Hawaiian shirt.

I think there are a lot of people who took this time off and now the hour to return to work is getting near. Both the home improvement center and the nursery had long lines of earnest weekend home improvement warriors trying to get one more home repair done before going back to the eight to five grind and drudgery. Or maybe they were using the gift cards received at Christmas, before the cards are misplaced or lost in the junk drawer.

I am on my way home from the overdue visit to the nursery and the local hardware store. I am taking a different route from the one I drove almost two hours ago, just exploring the different streets of the town. I have time to discover different routes home; no need to take the same streets I always drive during my daily commute to and from work. I am happy I found everything I needed for my gardening project. I am ready to be one of the eager weekend home improvement warriors, but I am more like an eager holiday gardener. I have in the trunk four bags of pebbles, four big bags of soil, a beautiful colorful planter plus four plain terracotta pots. I was surprised everything fit in the trunk. In the passenger seat there is a white mini rose plant, one pink armeria (thrift), a six pack of dianthus (pink), a plant of needle grass and a few other plants from the list that Emma and Bonnie recommended. I wanted a combination of native plants and low maintenance colorful plants. I have neither the time, patience nor green thumb to be manicuring my garden every weekend. I have been meaning to hide the bare spot in the front yard for a while and I tried planting a variety of flowers and grasses. When I asked Bonnie and Emma for their advice, their advice was to give it up. The prior owners tried everything and couldn't get grass to grow in that stubborn spot. Bonnie's words after seeing the disappointment on my face were: "Susy, buy some colorful pots and put them on top of some pretty pebbles or glass gems. You do not need to plant something on the stubborn spot to bring some life to it."

To my surprise, as I turn the corner onto Sea Foam Lane, I see the trunk of the yellow car opened and somebody bent over the passenger side. I park my car in the driveway, and before opening the door to get out, I send a group text to my friends, telling them the owner of the yellow car is back, just in case they are not already looking through their sheer curtains. I do not want them to miss the moment that they have been waiting for. What am I saying, the moment *we* have been waiting for. I must confess, every day I have been checking throughout the day if the car still there: when I get out of bed, when I am having lunch, before going to bed.

I get out of the car and open the trunk. I am trying to pull out one of the pebble bags. They are beautiful but heavy. The guy at the store made it look so easy when he lifted them and put them in the trunk as if they were pillows. He did one at a time, but still it looked effortless. If I cannot lift this bag, I will need to go inside and bring a bucket and take a few pebbles at the time. I position my body in the way you are told how to lift heavy things and I manage to get the bag out of the car. I am walking, hoping I am not injuring myself carrying this weight and I make it to the gate. Great, now how am I going to open it? I can barely carry the bag with both arms. I get as close as I can to the gate, trying to reach for the handle with the tips of my fingers. I feel how the bag is slipping from my shaking arms when trying to reach for the latch. The stranger turns around and sees me struggling. I only smile, hoping the effort of moving my lips doesn't distract the rest of my body from not letting the bag escape from my arms.

"Hey there, let me give you a hand." He quickly takes the bag from me. I think a few more seconds and the bag would have landed on my big toe.

"Thank you for saving me." I reply. I had been wondering who the car owner was, but I never put a face or imagined how he or she would be. He is tall with an olive complexion. His hair is cut short, and he is clean shaven. He is wearing a beige long sleeve polo t-shirt, a nice pair of denim pants, and spotless navy-blue canvas tennis shoes. When he turns around to ask me where I want the bag, I cannot help but notice his beautiful green eyes, framed by thick eyebrows.

"You can put the bag there by that patch of dirt." I

tell him, pointing at the stubborn barren spot. I feel like I am looking at him too intensely. I turn around to see if any of my friends have come out of their houses, to my surprise they are not anywhere to be seen.

"Do you have more bags you need to bring in?" He asks as he pulls the sleeves of his shirt up to his elbows. His forearms have the look of a guy that goes regularly to the gym.

"Yes, I do. I have three more bags of pebbles." I reply timidly while I am wishing I had ten bags. He goes to my car and starts bringing the rest of my goodies. He not only gets the pebble bags, but also the potting soil. He is carrying the bags with a smile and not worrying if his clothes are getting dirty. He doesn't say a word on any of the trips back and forth to the trunk of my car.

"Thank you, I appreciate your help. Then you are the owner of this yellow muscle car?" I ask the obvious when he is done bringing all the bags and pots to the barren spot.

"Yes, I am. I am the partial owner because I still have three more years to pay the bank for the car loan. Thank you for not towing it away."

"Well, to be sincere, one of my neighbors was considering calling the police to have the car towed away. But we discussed it among all the neighbors in the cul-de-sac and decided to wait a few days. It is the holidays and we thought maybe the car belonged to somebody visiting someone in the area. It would not have been nice for the owner to come back and find the car gone." I am telling him this while I am looking into his beautiful green eyes. I like that he is the kind of person that can look you in the eyes.

"I appreciate that you did not make the call to the police. It would have been one more drama to deal with during Christmas. My name is Adam by the way." He reaches over to shake my hand.

"My name is Susana, but everybody calls me Susy." I say as I shake his powerful hand.

"Do you like to be called Susy?" He asks. It is interesting, nobody has asked me that.

"Yes, actually I do. You are the first person that has asked me if I like to be called Susy." We both smile. And I say, "We had all kinds of theories about your car and the contents inside. One of my neighbors was convinced the car was stolen and the boxes were stolen goods." I am telling Adam all the stories we made up and he seems to be enjoying them.

"Wow, you guys have vivid imaginations! What was your theory, Susy?" Adam leans against his car waiting for my response. He is smiling and looking at me in a curious way.

"My theory was that the owner of the car was visiting, or in the process of moving houses or offices. He worked in an office, based on the nicely dry-cleaned white shirts, the black shoes and the tie. I did not think the car was stolen, or that the owner was living in it because the leather seats look new, and the exterior was impeccably clean. If somebody had stolen this type of car for a joy ride, most likely they would have burned some rubber all over town and it would not have been left in this condition." I am smiling as I finish telling my story.

"You are right, most days I work in an office when I am not in court. I am a lawyer. The boxes and bags in the trunk are some of my belongings that my ex-girlfriend tossed in the front yard when she decided to kick me out of my own house after I discovered she had been seeing her ex. She actually spent time with him in my place. I asked her to be gone before I was back from work. She told me she was not leaving, and I reiterated that I did not want to find her at the house that night. I came back and instead of finding she was gone, I found half of my wardrobe in the front yard lawn, with a few of my books and other items. She had the door locks changed while I was at work and I could not get into my own house. One of my neighbors gave me the boxes and bags to put my stuff in." He stops talking and his expression changes from serious to sad and angry. The type of expression I was wearing last year after breaking up with Taylor.

"I am sorry, you don't need to recount the story." I tell him and without realizing, I touch his forearm. I pull my hand away quickly.

"I am ok now, last week I was a mess. The day everything happened my childhood friend who lives just around the corner invited me to go with him to Arizona to visit his parents and get away from the drama. I just did not feel like staying at home to start putting back everything where it belongs. After some great family meals, hikes in the desert, shots of tequila and laughs with friends, I feel better. Now I just need to deal with the mess she left. I am sorry I am telling you all this." He puts his hands on his face and when he brings them down, he looks up at the blue sky.

"I don't mind. I went through a breakup last year. It got easier every day and one day the pain was gone. Too bad you need to go and deal with her after what sounds like a nice trip." I smile, running out of things to say and trying not to ask him something that will make him upset.

"Oh no, she is gone. The house is mine. She just had moved in with last summer. On the day she locked me out, I called her dad who is a prominent lawyer in the state and told him what she had done. He and his wife immediately came to pick her up and told me to send them the bill for everything she broke and damaged. Plus, any expenses incurred to get my place looking like it was before she had her tantrum."

"That's nice of her family." I reply, which sounds silly because money cannot delete the memories and pain of what he had gone through.

"I was sad and angry that she cheated on me, locked me out of the house, and broke some my family pictures. I went inside the house after they had left, I walked around the place making sure there was no water running, candles burning or anything that could damage my place further. Then as soon as the locksmith had changed the locks, I got out of there. It was already late, but my buddy invited me to spend the night at his place and the next day bright and early, we could start our road trip to Arizona. I locked the house, I drove around, came here and parked the car." He stops talking and looks around and continues. "You guys have a nice little street here. It has not changed at all, the trees have gotten bigger, and the color of the houses have changed, but for the most part it still looks the same."

"How do you know so well our little cul-de-sac?" I asked him to try to satisfy my curiosity.

"As a child I used to live in San Pedro. My father worked in the refinery. We lived two blocks away from here until one day dad got a job in Texas, and we left San Pedro. I came back to SoCal when I got a scholarship to one of the local universities. I haven't left the area since."

"It amazes me that you remember this street and left your car here."

"I used to walk these streets with my mom when she took me to kindergarten or the park, then going to school or visiting friends. Now if I am in court in Long Beach or here, I like to run from the park to the Point Fermin Lighthouse or the White Point State Park, before I go to hang out with my friend that just lives around the block."

"Then why you did not leave the car at your friend's house? Oh, sorry it is not my business." I can't believe I just asked him. I am being nosy.

"I parked it here because there is too much traffic on his street and I didn't want people looking at the contents of my car and getting tempted to break in." I just smile and he continues, "Hey Susy, by any chance do you have a black labrador?"

"Yes, I do. Why?" I turn around to see if Roland is visible from one of the windows, but nothing can be seen from the street.

"I think, I have seen you in the park tossing a ball down the hill for him to fetch it." He says. I can't believe he had seen me and I never have seen him. I better start paying more attention to my surroundings.

"Yes, that was me with Roland."

"You have a nice dog."

"Thank you, he is the best."

"I better get going, I am getting hungry, and I need to get home and clear the mess before I go back to work."

"Hey, would you like some homemade tamales? They are pork tamales with red sauce." The words just came out of my mouth. Now I am inviting him to eat tamales.

"I would love to take some. Did you made them yourself or buy them?"

"I made them. I used my grandma's family recipe."

"Are you sure you want to share them?"

"Yes, I am sure. Please take them off my hands. I can't eat more carbs for the rest of the year."

"Well, if that is the case, I sure would like to free you from the temptation of having them in your house."

"Great, just give me a minute." I run inside the house and let Roland go out the door. I want to see if he likes Adam. Roland seems to have better sense about men than I do. I am back with the last five tamales I had in the freezer. I hand over the container to Adam who is petting an over-exuberant Roland.

"Nice. Homemade tamales for lunch, thank you Susy. I will bring you the container back when I am in town, maybe on one of my runs to the park." He says as he gets ready to leave.

"There is no need, it is disposable." I say without realizing that maybe he wanted to stop by. Why did I have to open my mouth?

"Well, if you don't mind, I may just stop by to give you my opinion about your grandmother's recipe and see how your gardening project turns out. And to say hi to my buddy Roland." His tone of voice sounded playful and the sadness from a moment ago was gone. I know this from experience: those moments when we start forgetting about the pain, they are so wonderful.

"Wow, now the pressure is on, I have to turn that lifeless corner into something spectacular."

"Yes, I will be back to inspect it."

"Ok, Adam, see you around. Good luck with your place and thank you for helping me with the bags of pebbles." We wave goodbye as he turns around. Roland is next to me moving his tail, a clear sign he likes Adam.

"See you soon Susy." He tells me as he winks and gets in his car. The engine starts running and the sound of all the horses under the hood overtakes the cul-de-sac. He makes a 360 without burning the tires. I am sure it has been the most exciting driving maneuver that this street has seen in years, maybe decades. He stops at the corner and the right blinker flashes. The contrast of the red with the yellow paint looks amazing, and then he is gone. Would he be back one day to park his car? I hope so.

My phone is vibrating. Lesley and Miriam are texting me. Bonnie and Frances are coming out of their houses. I know they want to hear all the details from my conversation with Adam. They are walking towards my house.

"Ladies, if you want to know more about the handsome owner of the mysterious yellow car, you need to join me for lunch because I am famished." I tell them before they have a chance to ask me their first question.

"Yes, let go," Frances answers right away.

"I am going to ask Emma if she wants to go. But I am going regardless of what she says." Bonnie says as she turns around to fetch Emma.

"I will text Miriam and Lesley and ask them if they want to go." I text as fast as I can. Immediately I get a yes from both.

Emma comes back with Bonnie. Frances is closing the door to her cottage. Miriam is walking briskly out of her house, and I have taken Ronald inside the house. Lesley is pulling out of the garage. We are taking her SUV; her vehicle it is the biggest on the block, perfect for the six of us.

It is a wonderful winter day to go to the café overlooking the marina. A wonderful day to enjoy fresh fried calamari, drink a few mimosas, see the day fishing boats come and go with the hopeful fisherman, and the seagulls walking around. All this while we begin talking about the yellow mystery car and Adam.

We are six curious women stepping out of our little world at Sea Foam Lane to share a delicious lunch and some gossip!

THE END

RECIPES

$\mathcal{D}$ear Reader,

Thank you for having bought my book. I wanted to do something special with my first novella in the "Sea Foam Lane" series. Besides talking about food in the story, I wanted to share with you my family recipes.

I consider a recipe the framework for the preparation of a dish. Why? Because depending on our personal taste, allergies, preferences, budget and ingredient availability, we may decide to increase or decrease an ingredient, add an ingredient, or remove one. You are the chef in your house, and you decide what to add or remove.

You will notice in my list of ingredients that some of the quantities are ranges. I did this because you will need to decide how much you would like to add. For example, if I say one to three serrano chiles it is because I do not know if the chiles you buy will be extra hot or not. I do not know if you like spice food or not. I learned to add chiles to sauces and salsas, one at the time until they achieve the desired spiciness and flavor.

I consider cooking a creative process. Be creative! Life it is too short not to try different flavors.

Enjoy!

143

EVA HERNÁN

NOTES BEFORE YOU START COOKING

When handling peppers to remove seeds and stems you may want to use a fork and knife to handle them or wear gloves. I usually use a fork and knife when cutting hot chiles because I discover it is not fun trying to remove contact lenses at night.

Depending on the altitude of where you live cooking times will vary.

Seek medical help in case of burns. The use of potatoes and onions to treat minor burns is only a comment in this work of fiction, please do not attempt at home. This should not be considered as a medical advice. Seek medical help in case of burns.

POZOLE VERDE WITH CHICKEN BREAST

Ingredients for the chicken and the broth:

- 2 bay leaves
- 1/2 onion
- 1 serrano chile
- Black pepper
- Fresh Garlic
- 2 chicken breasts with ribs and skin (cut in quarters or halves it doesn't matter)
- Water

- In a pot put the chicken and add water until there is at least an inch of water above the chicken.
- Add the rest of the ingredients.
- Bring it to a boil and let it simmer until the chicken is tender. Approximately 30 – 40 minutes, depending on the size of the breast and how long is boiled vs. simmered.
- Let it cool down and then put it in the refrigerator, ideally overnight to get most of the fat condensed on the top, it will make the removal easier.

Note: You can skip this step if you remove all the skin and visible fat from the chicken breasts.

- Next day when you are ready to prepare the pozole, remove the condensed fat from the broth. Remove the chicken breasts.
- You can pass the broth through a strainer to make sure any loose pieces of bone or the bay leaves do not make it to the pozole.
- Shred the chicken breast by hand and toss out the skin and bones.

Ingredients for the green sauce:

- ½ to 1 onion
- 1 to 3 Serrano chiles. Depending on the level of spiciness desired.
- 10 oz of tomatillos.
- Broth, serrano and onion from boiling the chicken breasts
- 2 25oz. cans of hominy
- 1 can of jalapeño chiles
- ½ to ¾ bundle of cilantro. It depends on the size of the bundle and your taste for cilantro

- Peal the onion and tomatillos.
- Rinse the onion, serrano chiles, tomatillos and cilantro.
- Open the cans of hominy, discharge the liquid from the cans and then rinse the hominy.
- Open the can of pickled jalapeños.

Note: If you are concerned about the spiciness of the dish, then remove the seeds from the serrano and jalapeños.

- Place the boiled onion, boiled serrano, cilantro, tomatillos, jalapeños and some broth in the blender and blend them until it is a sauce.
- Taste and determine if you would like to add more serrano and jalapeño chiles.
- Add ¼ cup of pickle juice from the jalapeños can plus the number of chiles you would like, and blend some more.

You are almost done!!!

- In a pot put the rinsed hominy, the shredded chicken and the sauce.
- Bring it to a boil and then let it simmer for 30 minutes.

Garnish with slices of radishes, chopped onion and cabbage if desired. Add lime or lemon juice to your bowl. Salt to taste.

Sometimes I like to cook the pozole the day before I am planning to eat it to let the flavors meld.

PORK TAMALES IN RED SAUCE

I would recommend pork loin for the tamales, there is no trimming of fat or connective tissue. My second option is pork shoulder. I personally like to buy ½ or one slab of pork ribs to cook with the meat for the tamales. It is not needed, but I believe it provides extra flavor to the filling. I DO NOT put the ribs in the tamales, I eat them as a snack when waiting for the tamales to be ready.

You will need:

- 1 bag of 10 – 14 oz of corn husks to wrap the tamales
- Rinse husks and put to soak in hot water. When ready to make the tamales, drain them.

Ingredients for the filling:

- 2 pounds of pork loin or pork shoulder cut into small pieces
- 2 or 3 tablespoons of vegetable or corn oil

- 10 Ancho chiles. You may also find them as Ancho peppers, same thing just different words
- 4 Guajillo chiles (Guajillo peppers)
- Garlic powder or garlic cloves. For this amount of meat, I use 4 - 6 garlic cloves or ½ teaspoon of garlic powder
- ¼ teaspoon of cumin
- Salt and pepper
- Water

Red Sauce

- If you want to play it safe, remove the seeds from the dry peppers and wash them. Otherwise just cut the stem and wash them.
- Put the chiles in warm water to soak for 10 – 15 minutes. Make sure to submerge them in the hot water.
- When the chiles are soft put, them in the blender with the cumin and garlic.
- Add chicken broth or water until sauce consistency is achieved.
- Add the sauce to the meat when it has been seared and half cooked.

Meat

- In a large hot skillet (or frying pan) put the oil and the meat.
- Sear the meat and cover the skillet with a lid to keep the moisture in.
- Check the meat in 5 to 10 minutes to make sure is not getting stuck to the skillet. If there are not enough drippings from the meat, add a ¼ cup of water and cover.

- Before adding the sauce, cook the meat for 20 minutes.
- Add the red sauce and cook for at least 30 minutes.
- After the meat is cooked, remove the ribs if you added them.

Ingredients for the masa:

- 1 ½ cups of vegetable or corn oil.

Most tamale recipes call for lard. I do not use lard. My grandma would be horrified if she knew I do not use lard. Do NOT use olive oil unless you love the flavor. I use light olive oil and I can't taste the flavor in the tamales.

- 6 cups of corn flour.

There is some corn flour specially for tamales but is not a big deal if you cannot find it. I looked online and the price was too high compared to the regular corn flour for tortillas. I have prepared tamales using regular corn flour and corn flour for tamales and I do not recall any significant differ-ence between the two.

- 3 teaspoons of baking power
- 5 – 6 cups of water or chicken broth
- In a large bowl add the flour, the oil and the baking powder and 4 cups of water. I use my hands to start mixing the ingredients, it is an arms workout, but it is fun.
- If you can still see dry loose flour and if the mix is breaking, add more water.
- If the mix is still dry and is not sticking together and you cannot form a nice ball with it, add a little more water and mix.

- When you achieve the consistency desired, then start making tamales!!!

Tamale Preparation

- Put a small amount of masa in the center of a husk, a little bigger than a ping pong or golf ball. Use first the bigger husks, they are easier to handle and fold. The wider part of the just should be closer to our body.
- Spread the masa using the back of a spoon of a spatula.
- Add pieces of the meat in red sauce.
- Fold one side of the husk over the middle, then the other side, and the top toward the bottom.
- Placed them in a big steamer.
- After having placed the last of the tamales in the steamer, put two layers of corn husks on top to cover them, cover the steamer and cook them for 45 to 60 minutes.
- The tamales are ready when the husk detaches from the masa easily.

I start checking the tamales at the 45-minute mark, and if not ready I cook them additional 5 minutes and check again. I do this until they are cooked.
Enjoy!!!

NOTES

4. COOKING WITH MEMORIES

1. Seek medical help in case of burns. The use of potatoes and onions to treat minor burns is only a comment in this work of fiction, please do not attempt at home. This should not be considered as a medical advice. Seek medical help in case of burns.
2. The use of potatoes and onions to treat minor burns is only a comment in this work of fiction, please do not attempt at home. This should not be considered as a medical advice. Seek medical help in case of burns.

ACKNOWLEDGMENTS

Margaret thank you for having helped me to edit the first manuscript of my first short story that I ever wrote. I am sure you were horrified that I was considering writing.

Mr. William Linus, I will be always grateful for editing the multiple drafts of this story. I do not know what I would have done without you. Also, thank you for tasting the recipes included in this book.

To Jackie for reading the short story that was the inspiration for writing this novella. Thank you! Cheers!

Veronica Collado, my Spanish editor extraordinaire. Vero from my heart, thank you, thank you, for shaping up my Spanish manuscripts. You ensure Spanglish is not to be found in my books.

To my parents, for making difficult and selfless decisions in order to ensure my brother and I had access to the best education possible.

To my dear husband of 20 plus years, thank you for moral support in all my endeavors. Without you I would not have been able to accomplish what I have. You have been there in the bad, the good and the ugly.

To my forever friends, the ones which I enjoyed having tacos, pizzas, tortas and gorditas with, then going to dance for hours on a Thursday night and getting home at 2:00 a.m. to eat leftovers and then do the impossible. Wake up a few minutes before class to run up the alley and make it to the first class of the day, at 7:00! Yes, those were the days when we studied hard and played harder.

To my favorite USC Trojan for being willing to go on culinary expeditions and enjoy my home cooking. You my dear are an honorary Mexican. Moments become magical with you!

ABOUT THE AUTHOR

Eva considers herself fortunate for having spent time in her grandmothers' kitchens, learning about the different ingredients of traditional Mexican dishes like mole, tamales, carnitas, enchiladas, and many more.

During the second half of her childhood, she lived in a small rural community in central Mexico and witnessed firsthand the concept of farm to table. In Eva's case it was more like from field to table or chicken coop to table.

Eva is a graduate from the Universidad de Guanajuato and obtained an advanced degree from the University of Southern California.

She is the master chef in her house, and lives with her husband (experienced food tester and critic) in the Arizona high desert.

Eva enjoys cooking dishes that allow for leftovers, watching sunsets, and occasionally sunrises.

Visit her at *www.evahernan.com*.